THE LIST

FLORIAN DENNISSON

1

"**I** killed them all!"

The man who had just spoken these words was thin, and his emaciated face – sharpened by sunken cheeks and dark circles under his eyes that seemed to devour his entire face – showed evidence of poor health. The policeman on duty had raised, bushy eyebrows and instinctively brushed his palm against his service weapon.

The stranger walked slowly into the room, and with each step the officer tightened the grip on his SIG Sauer.

The visitor's eyes were bloodshot, and his clothes, with holes and yellow stains, made him look like a homeless person. His long, sleek black hair conveyed quite the opposite.

A pungent smell almost made the policeman recoil as this strange individual found himself leaning against the imposing block of wood serving as a lobby desk.

"I killed them all," he repeated, more softly this time.

The young man had already seen it all. However, on that morning of the first day of spring, he instinctively knew that the story that was being written before his very eyes was going to surpass all others.

It was a matter of keeping his cool and behaving like the professional that he was.

"Sir, do you care to be more specific, please?" he said, addressing the stranger in a neutral tone while keeping his right hand close to his weapon.

The man's eyes slowly closed, as if expressing a sense of relief, then he spoke again, almost inaudibly, "I killed them all..."

The sentence had slipped out of his mouth like a murmur of death, and the policeman had to suppress a grimace at the putrid breath of his interlocutor. Still in disbelief, he moved slowly to the side and went around the counter to come closer to the man. Each of his gestures were calculated, meticulous; tightening his grip on his gun, ready to draw in case of trouble.

But the man seemed exhausted, and the words he was repeating over and over again sounded like a final confession before his last breath.

"I'm going to approach you," the cop said calmly, "and you're going to have to show me your hands. It's protocol."

As soon as he finished speaking, the stranger, now docile and calm, stretched out his arms and brought his wrists towards him.

The scene became more and more bizarre.

The policeman glanced at the strange man and figured he was a junkie. He had everything of the heroin addict who would have mixed his daily fix with some form of psychedelic drug.

When the hands of the stranger were cuffed behind his back, the cop ordered him to follow.

The two men entered a cramped room with walls lined with photos and scribbled papers. Another officer sat behind a workstation crumbling under mounds of files; he looked up as they passed. Looking jaded, he briefly raised his eyebrows as the sole sign of communication between him and his colleague. He only showed some interest when the weird man was being interrogated.

"Explain it to me. Who did you kill, sir?"

The man lowered his face and the harsh neon light above him deepened his features, making him look menacing. He took a deep, trembling breath and repeated softly, "I killed them all."

"Okay," said the officer, "but who? You didn't come all the way here for nothing, did you? So, tell it all."

A heavy silence filled the room.

The stranger's eyelids slowly closed and he muttered the same words.

The officer turned his head to face his colleague, who mouthed a mute *"junkie"* with his lips. He let a few seconds fly by and continued in a tone that he wanted to sound kind and calm: "Take all the time you need, but you're gonna have to explain."

The man lifted his face and narrowed his gaze on a notepad sitting above the mess of the desk. He pointed to a pen with a quick flick of his chin and the policeman finally understood. "You wanna write it down? You a righty?"

He nodded slowly.

Judging the stranger to be calm and co-operative, the officer agreed to free his hand so that he could use the pen. His handwriting was erratic and shaky, and when he was done, he slid the sheet of paper towards the policeman.

On it appeared four names. A list. A list of four persons.

"Are these the people you killed, sir?"

Another silence.

"I killed them all!" repeated the strange man as a tear dropped from the corner of his eye.

2

———

Before his alarm went off, a clutter of cats jumped on Detective Michael Monroe's bed, expressing their craving of a good meal with friendly meows and purrs. One of them, a ginger cat with shaggy fur, came near his face and began to lick it with its raspy tongue.

The unpleasant sensation made Michael wince and he sat up.

"All right, all right. You're all going to eat!"

High-pitched meows instantly bounced about the bedroom walls.

Michael climbed out of bed and made his way down a narrow wooden staircase to the floor below. The cats followed him and when he opened a cupboard and grabbed a can of cat food, two of the feline horde leaped onto the kitchen counter. He filled up bowls of various sizes and shapes with their daily rations, and arranged them in a line on the floor.

He softly chuckled as he watched these furry friends – most of whom he didn't know the names of – noisily chow down.

He much preferred the company of animals and felt that the ingratitude with which cats are saddled – wrongly, in his opinion – was at least equivalent to that of their human counterparts.

Michael returned upstairs and hurried to the back of his room, to a narrow window that offered a breathtaking view of Lake Ontario. Almost stuck to the glass pane, an astronomical telescope stood there, firmly fixed on a tripod.

A trained observer would have noticed that the incongruous angle at which it was oriented did not allow him to look at the sky, let alone the stars.

Michael approached it and pressed his eye into the viewfinder for a few seconds. A furtive grimace of disgust passed over his face like a dark cloud in a storm, then he raised his head and made for the bathroom.

After a quick breakfast, he spent a few minutes petting the cats and finally left his house.

A cold wave had hit the state of New York – and more particularly the Lake Ontario area – and that first day of spring mostly looked like the beginning of winter. The chirping of blackbirds and thrushes were the only clues to identify the season.

Michael's footsteps crunched on the gravel as he walked to his car when he suddenly heard a voice behind him: "Going back to work?"

Michael turned around. A little old lady with a wrinkly face and blue-gray hair stood on his front step, hunched over a cane firmly anchored to the ground. She wore an old-fashioned green apron, and her posture made her look more vulnerable than she actually was. When she opened her mouth, all the doubts about her supposed frailty were cleared on the spot.

Michael wanted to smile, but the knot that had been

tightening in his guts since he'd woken up earlier that morning prevented him from doing so.

"Sorry, I'm late," he said, "but don't worry, I wired you the rent yesterday."

"That's not what I asked," she replied with a slight grunt.

He did his best to make his face as friendly as possible. "Well, yes, I'm going back to work today."

"You're abandoning me then? Men are all alike! I've been getting used to your presence all these weeks."

"I need to make the rent."

"Pretty smart," she said.

Michael waved at her and turned back when she called again: "By the way, your little buddy is back, and he almost broke the windowpane with his beak!"

"The crow?" he asked, frowning.

"Raven, crow, what do I know! But if you keep on taking care of all the animals around here, this place will become a real zoo pretty soon! It's bad enough with all these cats..."

He was relieved to realize that the bird, whose wings he had been working so hard to heal against the advice of the vets, was able to fly again. For almost a month, he had taken care of this crow, fed it, cleaned its wounds and changed its bandages daily, until one morning it disappeared. He'd figured that a tour outside had gotten the better of it or that it had been caught by a bird of prey. But then, two weeks later, his bird patient had come back for food.

"Is he still here?" Michael asked.

"Well, no! He flew out as soon as I raised my walking stick."

She was replaying the scene in front of Michael, but he wasn't fooled. The old landlady's words had been contradicted by an involuntary reflex of her face, the meaning of which he immediately identified.

As a freshly minted *synergologist*, Michael was an expert in the art of deciphering non-verbal language. A rise of the right eyebrow meant that the speaker disagreed with what he or she was saying.

Even though she had verbally expressed her dislike for the crow, her subconsciously controlled facial tics proved to Michael that she didn't hate the bird all that much. Her dislike for it must have been more a result of local folk beliefs – which attributed an ominous aura to the bird – than any real antipathy.

"Have a nice day," Michael finally concluded as he turned back to his car.

Once inside, the knot in his stomach became more uncomfortable, and he allowed himself to pause for a deep breath before starting the engine.

A green landscape of blooming trees and tall grass fields flashed before his windshield, while in his rearview mirror, the jutting silhouette of the mountains in the distance was visible. Bucolic and soothing scenery that did not succeed in calming the anguish caused by his return to the police station.

Sixty-three days and two hours. Michael had precisely counted the time that had elapsed since he left, like a prisoner would do by marking the walls of his cell.

Officially, his leave was merely time off after a burnout, but he and his captain at the time knew that it was more of a layoff than a short convalescence. Besides Michael, Captain Saget and Detective Emma King were the only two people who knew the real reasons for this forced break.

Built along a large avenue that led straight to the city center, the Rochester police station stretched for nearly four hundred yards and housed four buildings. It had received a recent facelift, and the façades had been repainted in more contemporary tones than the previous ones, which dated from the seventies.

This welcome visual refreshment made the station more appealing and somewhat less austere, but despite the efforts made, Michael's apprehension did not diminish.

He tried to park in his usual spot, only to notice with bitterness that another vehicle was already there. He drove around the parking lot again and passed the police station, whose large windows gave him a glimpse of the activity inside. His heartbeat quickened, and when he stopped the car, he closed his eyes and began breathing exercises. The mild anxiety attack quickly dissipated and he finally decided to get out of the vehicle.

The day before, the psychiatrist – whom he had been seeing once a week for the duration of his leave – had given him the green light to return to work. She had also prescribed anti-anxiety medication, which he had refused to use until a few days before his comeback, when the stress of returning to the station had become more and more uncomfortable.

As he walked up the flight of stairs to the main entrance, Michael suddenly wondered if his colleagues had been notified of his return. The thought caused his stomach to lurch again, forcing him to slow his progress and take a deep breath through his nose before pushing open the heavy glass door.

At the front desk, an officer looked up and, when he recognized Sergeant Monroe, put on a happy face.

A young woman with red hair gathered in a braid passed quickly in front of him, then turned round abruptly. Her azure-blue eyes lit up and a big smile crossed her face, enhancing the cloud of freckles that mottled her cheekbones.

Detective Emma King ignored protocol and threw herself around Michael's neck. Unaccustomed to affectionate gestures, he remained stiff and motionless, not knowing what to do with his arms. Fortunately, the hug lasted only a few seconds, and Emma pulled herself together. She tucked a lock of hair behind her ear and said: "Back at last, Sergeant?"

She had never really called him that; maybe in the early days when they had known each other, but, apart from official ceremonies and a few very specific circumstances, no one in the police station called each other by their rank. Michael took it as an attempt to lighten the mood. It didn't work, but he saluted the effort and offered his colleague a cold tap on the shoulder.

"We have a little something planned. Come," she said. They walked past the large open space – which was the nerve center of the station – and Emma gestured to the crowd.

Michael recognized everyone. Almost.

In the distance, behind what had always been his office, a tall blond man with angular features and a muscular body stood staring at him like a wolf sizing up a newcomer to the pack. Emma introduced him: "Michael, this is Lieutenant Boris Pavlowski. He's the one who filled the void when you left." She winked at him and Michael reached out to his superior.

Boris had brought the musky scent of his aftershave with him, and Michael could detect in the heady mix the scent of his perfume and deodorant.

A man who wears too much perfume is afraid of death, he thought.

The smell made him almost dizzy, but he put on a brave face in front of the colossus and gave him an affable smile. As expected, Boris's grip had proved far too strong, and when he spoke to Michael to give him a word of welcome, he scraped his Adam's apple, which the seasoned synergologist analyzed as a basic gesture of affirming superiority.

Message received.

After warm and friendly greetings that made Michael feel a little more comfortable, all the policemen headed to the lounge. When the door opened, he finally understood why.

Bottles of soda and appetizers were laid out on a table at the back of the room, and a cloth banner had the words "Welcome Back" in red letters.

Michael smiled hesitantly. Finally, he was beginning to relax.

As Sergeant Alsayed approached the buffet and went for a tray of snacks, Emma ran over and shouted: "Hey! Don't touch! Those are vegan snacks for Michael."

"Well, at least I know there's no pork in them!" said Jamal, his mouth full.

Michael appreciated his colleague's attention and smiled inwardly. He had always had to fight to get his fellow police officers to understand his specific diet. No meat, no fish, no eggs, no milk, nothing that was, as a rule, of animal origin. The reason why he didn't eat steaks, omelets or sushi had made its way into the minds of even the most skeptical; but when it came to dairy products and, worse, honey or seafood, jeers and sardonic comments quickly resurfaced. His life ethic was simple: he couldn't bear the idea of making any animal suffer for his own gustatory pleasure.

The anti-anxiety pills he had swallowed in the morning had made his mouth dry, and he felt relieved when he could drink a big glass of sparkling water before being assailed with questions and forced to offer explanations regarding his absence.

But Michael barely had time to finish his first sip when a too-familiar voice burst into the room, causing a slight unpleasant shiver to run down his spine. "I'm sorry to cut your little party short, but we have a custody transfer in a few minutes, and it's a pretty serious matter. Everyone, to the briefing room!" said the boss in an authoritative tone.

Captain Assia Jenkins, newly in command of the Rochester

police station, had burst into the room and glared at Michael, before leaving as abruptly as she had entered.

It felt as if his heart had just skipped a beat. The reason for the knot tightening in his stomach had suddenly taken shape.

Jenkins's predecessor, Henry Saget, had put in place a new way of working – after a stint with the Swedish police. Walls were torn down and office spaces were brought together in one large room with the aim of creating synergies and opportunities amongst the policemen of the station. Today, open spaces are commonplace throughout the world, but in the eighties, the initiative was rather innovative – or viewed as a heresy, depending on which side of the force you were on.

Yet that indiscriminate way of running things was the reason behind the resolution of famous cases in the area, due to the emulation it generated.

As Michael entered the room, he realized that Lieutenant Boris Pavlowski had been given his office and had obviously taken over from him in his usual pairing with Emma.

The vacant desktop he was contemplating before him was obviously his new workspace.

Assia Jenkins did not bother to wait until he was seated to begin her speech. "A few hours ago, a man presented himself at the Bloomfield police station, stating that he had killed several people. He refused to give his identity, but produced a list of four names which, according to the officer who took his deposition, would constitute his four victims. His fingerprints were run through the IAFIS with no result and, apart from a bus ticket and some sort of business card, the search yielded nothing. The DA has ordered the custody transfer and we will have him here in a few minutes."

She paused for a moment and looked at the audience, which was plunged into a disciplined silence, carefully avoiding Michael's gaze.

He could not help but observe her in great detail. Her skin was the charming color of caramel, and the delicate shape of her face softened the stern look which her long black hair, slicked back in a neat ponytail, was giving her. From where she stood, her endless legs made her look very tall. No doubt she must have made quite an impression among the heterosexuals of the station when she took her position. Yet Michael studied the audience's reactions and everyone remained impassive, as if absorbed in the speech.

Good job imposing yourself as the boss, Assia, he thought.

"Alsayed and Almeida, Fischer will assist you; take care of the first warrants. King and Pavlowski, you go in the field. We have a video conference with the DA in about an hour: let's try to glean everything we can by then."

She turned on her heels and disappeared down the corridor to her office.

A slight feeling of unease had suddenly settled over the cops in the open space. No one had said anything, but silence sometimes spoke louder than words. Captain Jenkins had not assigned Michael to any mission; a fact that everyone noticed. Did she feel that, given the reasons for his recovery, it was still too early to put him on such a serious case? Or was it simply the manifestation of a more personal vendetta?

Emma's familiar voice cut through the flow of his thoughts. "So much for your little homecoming," she said apologetically.

"No worries."

"Still as talkative as ever, I see. Your leave did you good!"

In other circumstances, Michael would have been keen to display a little smile, but her humorous attempt did nothing: the knot in his belly turned little by little into a ball of anger.

Emma put a friendly hand on his shoulder. "I'm investigating a streak of stolen motorbikes if you and your big brains want to have a look at it," she said.

She had always teased him about his obsession with synergology and the art of deciphering micro-expressions and body language. For her, as for most of the other policemen, there was no substitute for a good old confession or hard evidence. She swore by DNA and cell phone data. Michael was no stranger to these new technologies, but for him, man was still a complex animal that needed the expertise and the scrutiny of his fellow human beings. No computer worth its salt could fathom the complexities of the human mind as well as the people who had learned the proper techniques. Synergology and the study of non-verbal communication were as powerful as an entire forensics team.

"You don't dig it?" she went on as he didn't show any sign of a reaction. "You know–"

"Emma!" shouted Boris Pavlowski with his stentorian voice from the back of the room. "May we get started, please?"

The young woman stiffened and her expression changed. She sighed quietly and turned around to head for her workstation.

Checking out his new desk with a nervous glance, Michael reached out and grabbed Emma's wrist before she pulled away. "Check and see if Pavlowski has my Rubik's cube somewhere in his drawers, will you?"

She nodded indifferently and continued walking.

The vast open space was coldly lit both by the neon lights from the ceiling and the unpredictable and changing outside glare, coming in from large windows. Michael liked to lose his gaze in the foliage of the big trees that lined the main avenue alongside the station, or in the cotton of the clouds that seemed to cling to the mountaintops in the distance, like shipwrecked sailors adrift. On that first day of spring, temperatures were breaking records below seasonal norms, and the mountains were clothed in a snowy blanket, fueling dubious jokes from climate change deniers. Man had indubitably screwed up his environment, but the spectacle was no less magnificent.

Suddenly, a police van driving towards the station cut through his field of vision. Two officers got out of it, and went around the vehicle to the back doors. They helped a tall, dirty-looking man out of the van. He looked as if he hadn't slept in days, like a homeless person, but something stood out in his messy appearance: the man was clean-shaven.

Soon the group was joined by Captain Assia Jenkins. Michael looked into their faces, and tried to read their lips in order to make out the details of their conversation from a distance. He didn't get much out of their facial expressions and gestures, but when his gaze turned to the man in custody, he could tell by his furtive glances around that he was afraid of something. He stood hunched over, and the slightest rumbling of an engine coming from afar startled him. His eyes were bulging and his pupils were fully dilated.

Michael had no doubts, this guy was scared.

3

The man was placed in the *fridge*, the strangest and most infamous cell in the station. Located at the end of a long and dimly lit corridor, the *fridge* had abnormally low temperatures, and its four concrete walls oozed with moisture. Many stories were told about why the place was so cold. For the more reasonable, the reason was a micro-leak from an old water pipe embedded in the wall that, over the years, had filled the plaster with water and made the room impossible to heat. For others, less Cartesian, the evil reputation of this jail came from a prisoner who had killed himself there, his ghost still haunting the place.

The truth must have been somewhere in between, but the various chiefs who succeeded each other never deigned to undertake the necessary checks and work. This cell became convenient, and few were the culprits who didn't crack after two days of chattering teeth.

If the strange man was reluctant to give up his identity, it was a safe bet that the *fridge* would break his silence.

The few clues in this particular case had been divided up between the two investigation groups, and Alsayed, Almeida and Fischer were already working on the handwritten list. Four names, four potential victims. The three policemen knew they had to act quickly and so they made copies of the list and divided the work among themselves. Jamal was going to launch a search for Colin Vassard and Jenni Grosch-Steiner, while Almeida and Patrick were going to look after Tod Sheepmann and Slevin Bradich respectively.

Boris and Emma, as Group A, decided to leave their stranger in the cold for a while before conducting their first interview. For the time being, their efforts were focused on the bus ticket he had in his pocket.

The young woman consulted the bus lines that served stops near the Bloomfield police station – where the stranger had first gone – and found only one. In the rural areas around Rochester, the frequency of public transportation was much lower than in the city center, and if their suspect had arrived at the station at 8:12am, it meant he had taken the number 33 bus and gotten off at 8:08am.

She straightened and addressed Group B across the room. "Guys, I have something for you! Our man probably took the 33 towards Canandaigua Lake. I'll let you see the bus company in order to contact the driver who was working on this tour."

Almeida had just scribbled a few notes on a notepad and everyone responded with a thundering "Okay" in unison.

Emma swiveled in her chair and saw Boris looking at the only other item they had found in the stranger's pockets. A simple white rectangle, the size of a business card, with a logo printed in black: the letter G in bold type, in the center of a thin isosceles triangle. He held the card up to his teammate and shrugged silently. In response, she shook her head negatively. No one seemed to recognize the pictogram.

From his desk, Michael could see his colleagues bustling around him and felt as useless as an observer watching the activity of an anthill. Feeling isolated, his thoughts turned to his former boss, Captain Henry Saget. With him, none of this would have ever happened; he would never have excluded an officer from a criminal investigation, let alone a possible quadruple homicide. But Assia Jenkins, who took charge of the station the day after Michael was put on leave, surely had her reasons.

I'm going to have to face her at some point, he thought briefly.

He looked down at his desk and the files piling up in front of him added a bitter taste to his return. His hands began to shake and he regretted not having found his Rubik's cube, because it was proving to be a rather effective remedy for his little bouts of anxiety. However, even the past sixty-three days and two hours that he'd spent on paid leave of his colorful puzzle would not have been enough.

He tried to forget about the anti-anxiety meds, and concentrated on his breathing and the cold sensation in his nostrils. With each breath, the waves of anxiety gradually dissipated. He had voluntarily left his box of painkillers in his car and refused to take them in public, even in case of an insurmountable panic attack.

"I think our guy is ready, don't you, Pavlowski?" said Emma, breaking the silence.

Boris raised his head above his screen and nodded. The two policemen left their desks together and disappeared from the open space.

The fridge had played its part indeed.

When they arrived at the cell, the stranger was curled up in the fetal position and shaking all over. Unlike the prisoners who had already experienced this particular jail, he did not cry out for a blanket or urge to be taken out. He just lay still and did not even look up when Pavlowski entered the room.

The lieutenant lifted him up with a manly gesture, and the man looked down at the floor, repeating his litany, "I killed them all, I killed them all!"

"All right, all right, you're going to tell us about it all, okay?" said Boris.

The man did not resist, and let Boris handcuff him and be led into one of the interview rooms.

Once settled, Emma positioned herself in front of the stranger and scrutinized him for a long time. Her partner was already running the software that allowed the interview to be filmed and recorded.

She held up a copy of the list of names and slid it across the desk, right in front of their man.

"These people, here," she indicated with her index finger, "it is you who killed them, correct?"

"Wait!" Boris said in an aggressive tone. Emma's eyes widened in astonishment as she turned to him.

"First, we have to make sure the webcam is working," he continued, softening his voice.

"Come on, it works! Let's do this already!" she replied impatiently.

Boris stopped fiddling with the computer and his face took on a serious look. "Emma, this is important. If there's a bug with the recording, you know very well that the interview will be worthless. It's already happened to me once, okay, and I don't want it to happen again!"

For a moment, the young woman considered his words and closed her eyes. Boris then understood that she agreed with him and went back to his tests. After a few seconds, he gave her the green light with a nod. The young woman sighed.

"Those names you wrote," she went on, "they are victims, right?"

The stranger stared into space, his eyes twitched as if wounded by thousands of tiny electric shocks. Every time there was a loud noise, he shuddered and turned around slowly as if he feared he was being attacked from behind.

"Were you alone when you did... that?"

A whisper, that damned phrase on a loop.

"How did you do it? How did you kill them all?"

The only answer he could give was always the same: "I killed them all."

After a few minutes, Boris scribbled some words on a loose piece of paper and passed it to Emma.

We won't get anything out of him. Back to the fridge?

She read the message and approved it with a slow blink.

The suspect suddenly seemed curious about what the two cops were hiding from him and looked at the sheet of paper.

Suddenly, he threw his head back, his face contorted into a grimace of terror. He tried to raise his hand to obstruct the webcam lens, but his shackles prevented him from doing so.

"You're with the captain, ain't that right?" he shouted. "You're with him! Tell him I killed them all! All of them!"

The man's eyes widened and he spasmed. Emma rushed at him and had to use all of her weight to hold him down in his chair. Pavlowski slapped the man's cheeks to snap him out of it.

A few seconds later, he finally calmed down and the police officers took him back to his cell. There, he seemed satisfied to go back to his fetal position, on the floor, in the center of the cell. He did not even ask for something to protect himself from the cold. He just lay there with his eyes closed, shaking like a dead leaf.

Back in the busy workroom, Emma and Boris approached Jamal and the rest of the investigation team.

"So?" Jamal asked.

"Nothing. The guy just looks like a junkie in the middle of a withdrawal," said the young woman, adjusting her long red hair into a braid that she made surprisingly quickly. "You?"

"Not much either. We've just been to all the rehab centers, hospitals, homeless shelters: nothing. Nothing from the IAFIS either; no file on him. We'll send an officer in an hour to speak to the driver of the bus in which he traveled, but we already had him on the phone; he remembers him, but not at what stop he got on."

Lieutenant Pavlowski stood a little apart, arms crossed.

"Cameras, maybe?" he said in an almost robotic voice.

"On the bus?" Jamal Alsayed retorted with a smile. "No, not on those, unfortunately. On the other hand," he continued, turning to his screen, "I should get the results from my inquiries towards social services, cell phone companies and such today."

"Okay," Emma concluded, "let us know as soon as they come in."

As they walked back to their desks, she waved to Michael, who replied with a cold, distant nod.

She then walked over to Boris's workstation and frantically searched through the drawers, while her partner looked on in amazement. When she finally found what she was looking for, she crossed the room in long strides.

"Here," she said, putting the Rubik's cube noisily in front of her ex-teammate. "Maybe you'll stop sulking?"

The air she had moved by approaching him carried the scent of a sweet vanilla perfume. Michael's olfactory senses immediately detected the new scent: she had changed her deodorant.

He reached for the cube-shaped puzzle and looked up at Emma. "Any progress?" he said in a neutral tone.

"Well, I'm fine thanks, and you? How have you been these last two months? What did you do? Vacations?"

She and Captain Saget were the only two people – besides Michael – who knew the real reason behind his paid leave. His little crisis was really just a full-blown burnout. Policemen, like firefighters, ER personnel and rescue services, were in the heart of the turmoil, in the eye of the storm, and were hit hard by all the villainy of human behavior. It took a lot of guts to deal with this flood of incivilities whose violence was increasing, the ever-growing lack of empathy and the ever-deepening despair that was eating away at humanity like a devastating cancer.

He hadn't taken a vacation – he would have liked to – and Emma, with her sardonic sense of humor, had stung him. Like everyone else in Michael's life, she was looking for a reaction from him; but he himself did not possess the key to the inner garden of his own soul. However, the sarcastic remark provoked a discreet chuckle that the young woman noticed immediately.

"What's the new guy like?" Michael asked.

"Pavlowski? Great; square, a little too much sometimes, but that's all that's expected of him, so I'm fine with it."

"And your case?"

"Ah, you finally came back to it!" she thundered. "I'm relieved. I thought you were going to ask me how I was." She winked and resumed, "Quiet as a church mouse... or more like a broken record. He keeps saying, 'I killed them all', and we have no idea who he is. Never ever seen that before. Four potential victims, a culprit who turns himself in, but won't say anything more."

"What was his demeanor when you interviewed him? His face, his expression..."

"Oh no, Mike. You're not going to go all brain tricks on me. We have nothing. If you ask me, he's just a junkie who's in withdrawal. With four potential victims, the DA has no other choice but to mobilize the whole task force, but honestly, I give us only a few hours before closing the case."

All of a sudden, Jamal Alsayed interrupted them from afar. "Sergeant King!" he said, perpetuating the local custom of calling each other by their rank and surname when business was getting serious. "We have something on one of the names on the list!"

Captain Assia Jenkins had given the green light to Group A, consisting of Emma and Boris, to go to Cobbs Hill, one of the more upscale parts of Rochester, and investigate.

A freezing rain was pouring on the city and pounding the windshield of their car. The defroster was no longer working, so Pavlowski was forced to wipe the windshield regularly in order for his colleague to see through it.

After about a twenty-minute drive, they arrived at a large building overlooking the lake. The bad weather did not do the place justice, but in normal conditions, the clear view made it possible to admire the green waters below and the mountain peaks in the background.

The investigators had found an electricity contract under the name of Colin Vassard and the matching address. Given the real-estate prices in the area of Cobbs Hill, Emma thought that the man they were looking for must have a job that paid well.

An automatic light went on when they arrived and guided them down the hallway to the presumed victim's door. A gold plaque read "Colin A. Vassard" and confirmed they were at the right place.

The young woman rang the doorbell several times. No answer.

"Mr. Vassard?" she shouted, "Rochester police, open up please!"

Still nothing.

She drew her weapon and nodded to her teammate. "Mr. Vassard," Emma said a little louder, "if you don't open the door, we'll have to break it down."

A minute passed in an oppressive silence, and Emma, impatient with adrenaline, bent down and grabbed the breaching ram they had brought. Emma spat out a final warning and, with no response, kicked the door down.

Boris and her then entered the apartment of a man whose name was written in shaky handwriting on a mysterious list, among three others.

4

Boris and Emma had already been gone for an hour, and Michael was in a state of disarray. He had been assigned to deal with his overdue paperwork. A childish punishment that reminded him of the first hazing he'd endured in the army when he was a freshman.

His Rubik's cube had kept him busy for a few minutes – he'd finished it several times already – but as he watched Jamal and his colleagues being absorbed in their investigative work, he felt a slight tingle of impatience tickle his limbs.

Everyone had their noses glued to a screen or their ears glued to a telephone receiver. No one noticed that he had gotten up and was moving toward the jails.

If the police station looked stark to anyone entering it for the first time, that impression was even stronger in the wing that housed the cells: the ubiquitous concrete gave the decor a blood-curdling coldness, and at the end of a poorly lit, depressing hallway, the *fridge* was the worst of the lot.

Michael's footsteps echoed on the heavy metal doors lining the corridor and, at the sight of the one at the end, he slowed down.

He gently slid the peephole open and brought his face closer.

The stranger was curled up in the center of the room and showed no reaction. But all of Michael's senses were alert, and he could notice a slight acceleration in the man's breathing rate. He knew he was being watched.

Normally, Michael could detect tiny variations in the smell of perspiration that indicated stress and often, fear. He stuck his nose into the gap of the peephole, but the sweat secreted by the suspect's apocrine glands was so strong that it overwhelmed any of his attempts to analyze it. This guy obviously hadn't bathed in days.

Emma was probably right, he was, after all, a junkie who, in the delirium of withdrawal, had made up this murder story so that he could be taken care of and treated. Yet something deep inside the detective told him that the case had to be examined beyond simple appearances.

If this stranger's confession was a fabrication for the sole purpose of being taken care of by public health services, why had he gone so far as to imagine a list of four victims? Their names were far too specific to be mere lies.

Michael continued to observe the suspect for several minutes. He wished he could have sat across from him and questioned him. Since he had graduated from his synergology training, every victim interview, every suspect interrogation, or filing of a report was different. He directed his questions, scrutinized the smallest of reactions and analyzed every twitch of the face or hands. The devil is in the details, even the most insignificant ones.

One day, when he was taking the simple testimony of a

young woman whose husband had been killed on a motorcycle, he noticed that she slightly raised her right eyebrow when she mentioned her deceased husband. In her own words, she described her man as loving and caring, while her non-verbal language expressed the opposite. Her speech didn't match what she was thinking deep inside. Michael decided to dig a little deeper and focused his questions on the husband's behavior. It only took a few minutes for the poor widow to burst into tears and admit that her husband had beaten her.

The devil is in the details.

"Are you cold? Do you want a blanket?" said Michael, his voice breaking the silence of the *fridge*. The stranger began to mumble inaudible words. The policeman listened and understood.

"I killed them all, I killed them all..."

It seemed that the poor bastard kept repeating this sentence like an ominous mantra, as if stuck in a hellish loop whose only way out was death.

Michael would get nothing out of him. Not as long as he was out of the investigation and the alleged perpetrator was lying like a homeless man on the cold concrete floor of a cell. Michael had to come to terms with the fact that his burnout had taken its toll on him, and he would have to regain everyone's trust before he could be fully reinstated in the station. The most difficult part would be to eventually face Assia...

The main door to the cells slammed shut with a noise that startled him. A massive and swift shadow was moving quickly towards him. It was Boris.

"What the fuck are you doing here?" he thundered in his authoritarian tone.

He was caught red-handed. He was there, at the end of this soulless corridor, in front of the cell of the only person in custody in the whole precinct. No excuse would be valid.

Pavlowski immediately noticed that the peephole was open and frowned.

"You have no right to be here, Monroe!"

The racket had brought Assia out of her office. Pavlowski looked down and tried to leave silently but she was standing firmly in the doorway like Cerberus barring his way to the underworld.

"What's going on here?" she said to her lieutenant, deliberately avoiding meeting Michael's gaze.

Boris shrugged and put on his calmest voice. "Nothing, Captain, our man in custody was making some trouble," he lied.

Michael froze, his eyes fixed on his feet. Assia Jenkins paused before asking, "How did the search go?"

The tall blond man moved closer; Michael was now caught between the two. "Crime Scene are on site to sweep the place. We'll know more in a few hours, I guess, but for now, nothing new. The apartment was almost empty."

"I just got off the phone with the DA," she said, "he's making the trip here. Try to get something out of our suspect or find convincing clues; I feel that he is going to hand over the case to Major Crime if we have nothing by then."

She turned on her heels and disappeared from the field of vision of the two policemen.

In an icy silence, Boris passed his colleague and, as the narrowness of the corridor did not allow two people to stand side by side without brushing up against each other, he gave him a quick, light shoulder tap. He moved away a few inches, then turned around to face Michael, pointing an accusing index finger at him.

"Don't hang around here anymore, you understand?" he said.

Michael answered with a brief nod and waited for Pavlowski to return to his office before deigning to move.

He still wondered why the lieutenant hadn't inveigled him in front of Assia, their boss. Perhaps he had noted this faux pas in a corner of his memory, and was saving the appropriate retort for later?

Michael walked through the open space without anyone noticing his presence. Sometimes it seemed to him that he was just a lost soul, a ghost desperately looking for a way to the peace of heaven. True, he was not very talkative or affable, but he was clear about his own fate and knew that he could be a loyal and helpful friend, when he decided to put his trust in someone. He did not really participate in the social life of the barracks since he had chosen, in exchange for a significant reduction in his purchasing power, to live "amongst the civilians" and to move away from the nerve center of Rochester. It was undeniable that the esprit de corps made the policemen a very special category among their fellow humans, but, for him, the promiscuity and the almost non-existent private life did not make him a better cop, on the contrary. He needed peace and quiet, and solitude.

Only Emma had been able to break through Monroe's thick shell, and he was often angry at himself for forgetting that, apart from Henry Saget, she was his only friend.

Michael brushed past her desk and she smiled at him. "What did you do now?" she asked in an almost joking tone.

"I was just hoping to get a closer look at our suspect," he mumbled, stopping his walk to face her.

"Told you, a junkie. In half an hour, no more, he's shaking all over and begging us to give him a shot," she proudly predicted.

"He's already shaking…"

"That's because of the *fridge*. Wait a little and you'll see!"

He looked up and observed the young woman's workstation: pending files, a word-puzzle book, the photo of her twin brother, a pot overflowing with pens and their chewed-up caps, and the screen of her computer whose bluish light revealed the unique shine of her red hair.

One detail caught his eye. She noticed it. "What are you looking at?"

His pupils had dilated, and drops of cold sweat were already beading on his lower back. The adrenaline pumping through his body at the speed of his heartbeat made him dizzy. He struggled not to faint and sink into a whirlwind of abject memories, still buried deep inside himself. After a long minute, he finally found the strength to say a few words to Emma. "Where did you find this?"

"In the stranger's pockets. He had only this and a bus ticket."

Michael stood still, as if hypnotized by the black logo on a white background printed on the business card. He knew all too well this vile letter surrounded by this diabolical triangle: it was the symbol of the darkest hours of his life.

Was it a simple coincidence or a message intended for him, delivered by an obscure individual serenading a morbid litany?

The young woman, thinking that her colleague was perhaps on the verge of one of his panic attacks, reached out an arm and firmly grasped his shoulder. "Michael, are you okay?"

In response, he shook his head and snatched the small clear plastic bag containing the business card.

Before Emma had time to protest, he was already gone, out of the open space, and reaching the door to Captain Assia Jenkins's office.

He barely caught the bag that was slipping from his sweaty hands, took a deep breath and knocked on the wooden panel.

"Come in!" thundered Assia from inside.

With a slow but determined gesture, Michael opened the

door and found himself facing the woman who had avoided his gaze all morning.

The smooth, perfect brown face of the precinct's chief remained impassive, yet he detected microblinks in it. Bad sign.

He broke the silence with a calm voice. "I think I should be assigned to one of the investigation teams."

She seemed to digest the few words Michael had said, then took a seat behind her desk. "Close the door, will you?" she said, indicating the entrance with a nonchalant gesture.

He complied and approached her. Assia had not given him permission to sit down, so he put the evidence bag in front of her. "I have good reason to believe that I can get information about our man in custody."

"You just have to pass it on to Pavlowski or Alsayed," she said, her dark eyes holding his gaze.

"I know this logo, I know where our man might come from. We have four potential victims, we have to act quickly. Let me take part in the investigation."

"No way," she retorted without losing her composure. "If you have knowledge of elements likely to move the investigation forward, it is your duty to reveal them. You know what you expose yourself to if you don't do so? It's your first day back at the station, so don't waste it."

"Let me participate in the research!" he said in a firmer tone, which Assia noticed.

"You show up like this, as if nothing had happened, and you dare to ask me for a favor? You've just come back from a burnout, Michael, I refuse to involve you in such an important investigation, it's too early. We can't make any mistakes here, the facts are too serious if proven true."

He clenched his jaw which formed two bumps on either side of his thin face. He closed his eyes for a long time then swallowed with difficulty. "This is the logo of a cult," he said as calmly as possible, "a cult that I happen to know very well."

"So go to King and Pavlowski and tell them everything you know: I can't advise a better move."

There was a long, electric silence. Michael clenched his hands on the plastic bag, then inhaled sharply. "I lived in that cult for ten years, and I was rescued from it when I was fourteen. Everyone knows me there. Put me on this investigation, it's more than vital for its progress."

If his superior felt the slightest emotion at the mention of a past that obviously seemed to be painful, she did not show it. Her fine features remained marble. "And what makes you think you're more competent than anyone else in this matter?"

"They won't talk to anyone... except me."

Assia Jenkins considered for a few seconds what her detective had just said and sighed. "In that case, you will form a new team with Pavlowski," she said visibly reluctant, "and you will be under his command. King will join Alsayed's team. For the moment, you go to your superior and explain everything you know."

Michael was unable to express any sense of gratitude, for he felt no joy in being included in the current case. On the contrary, this assignment – which he had certainly asked for – had just opened a Pandora's box. He was going to have to dive back into the fog he had allowed to thicken away from him and confront old demons. Emma, the one who knew him best at the station and who, by her presence alone, managed to soothe him, would not even be at his side to face this ordeal. Had he just set up his downfall into Hell?

5

———————

The open space was bustling with activity, and the ambient hubbub, like the distant tumult of waves in an ocean still relatively calm before the storm, was occasionally interrupted by protests against anyone who had left the main doors open. Outside, the wind had picked up and the thermometer had plummeted, dropping the temperature below 40°F. The weather was so unusual that a request had been made to turn on the collective heating of the barracks, something that would have to go through the administrative channels and that would unfortunately be effective far too late, when summer would already be at the city's gates. Unless, of course, the climatic anomaly settled in time. Almeida and Fischer were talking about the pole reversal: they must have read some articles on dubious websites and, in any case, they knew nothing about it. They just regurgitated the mash they had been served, and often wrongly.

When a sudden draft came through the doorway, the nearest officers almost complained, but the slim figure of Captain Jenkins who appeared in the room cut short any protest.

She held a folder in her right hand, and the

disproportionately large watch that clasped her left wrist made it look as fragile as glass.

"Detective Monroe has some news about today's investigation," she told the audience. "You're going to reform three different groups: Pavlowski and Monroe in Group A, Alsayed and King, Group B and in support, Fischer and Almeida in Group C."

The two sidekicks winked at each other discreetly, and Emma was glad she was not with them. She felt a little bitter, though, because Michael, her longtime partner, would be away from her, in another group.

She loved her Mike deeply, not as a woman loves a man, but rather as a sister loves a brother. Emma had lost her twin during her teenage years and, even if her colleague had nothing in common with the laughing, delightful young boy that was Lucas, she had been able to detect in him the purity of soul that she found unique.

Of course, he had a rather cynical vision of the world, was full of quirks, wore a shell as hard as steel and didn't speak much, but the great fragility that he made a point of concealing from the eyes of all had won her over. If her heart wasn't only set on women, she would have liked a guy like Michael. He would have given her a hard time, but she would have fought to prove to him that the world was not always as it seemed.

Emma met her friend's gaze as he walked toward Boris's office and shrugged with a smile. In response, he gave a grin that looked more like a grimace of pain than anything else. She laughed inside.

Don't sweat it, Mike. Smiling is not your forte, she thought.

Boris nodded silently and arched his eyebrows, inviting his new teammate to start the conversation. Seeing that Michael, almost ignoring him, was busy with something else, he decided to break the ice. "You have new clues from what I hear?"

"I need you to take me to the first victim's house," Michael answered briefly, without turning around.

"Crime Scene are sweeping the place, we better move on to something else," he replied coldly.

As if Pavlowski hadn't spoken, Michael stood up abruptly, took a few steps towards his desk and grabbed the jacket that was hanging on the back of his seat.

"We can use my car if you want," he said, walking toward the exit.

Stunned by the audacity of addressing a superior in this way, Boris widened his eyes and sighed loudly. Emma, who had been watching the scene from afar, approached the tall blond and put a friendly hand on his shoulder. "Don't take it the wrong way, he's a bit cold and stubborn. You'll see, his ways are weird, but I assure you that it is effective."

He rose questioning eyes towards the young woman.

"Give him the benefit of the doubt and go back there. I know him, he needs to start this investigation from scratch."

Another sigh, almost a growl, and Pavlowski resigned himself to following Michael. "We're taking my car, but you're driving," he told Michael, tossing a set of keys across the room.

Back in Cobbs Hill, in Colin Vassard's apartment, Boris and Michael had put on full-body suits, hygiene caps and overshoes so as not to interfere with the careful work of the Crime Scene technicians. A few familiar faces greeted the detective, and

Pavlowski once again felt like a stranger in an unfamiliar country, his ridiculous attire not helping.

He had given in to the advice of the beautiful Emma, and when his colleague pulled out of his pocket a blindfold like the one they give out on planes, he regretted listening to her. *What the hell was this guy doing?*

"I need you to direct me to all the rooms and describe them to me," Michael said in a neutral tone, as if the request was trivial.

"Are you serious?" Boris whispered through his teeth.

One of the technicians there, busy taking pictures of the hallway, had reached out and, sensing Sergeant Boris Pavlowski's reticence, addressed him in the hope of reassuring him. "Is this your first time working with Detective Monroe? Don't worry, the method is weird, but it's bloody efficient."

Boris felt cornered, he clenched his jaws. Everyone was looking at him now and he was not a man to make a scandal in the middle of a crime scene. He had just been transferred to the county and, so to speak, he had fallen in love with Rochester, its crystal-clear lake and its majestic mountains in the background. If Monroe's song and dance were a local custom, he would not oppose it – for the moment – but one thing was for certain: he also had his ways, and he wanted to establish his authority within the precinct and to make the other cops respect him.

He closed his eyelids for a long time, as if to calm his nerves, then decided to put his two big hands on Michael's shoulders to guide him. "Well," he breathed, "the hallway, you've seen it, I think. We're heading to the back."

"What's on our left? It feels like there's a gap."

"There is a small staircase that leads to a single room on the lower floor, a bathroom," Boris answered in the most serene tone possible.

As if in a heavy and ungainly ballet, the two men slowly

progressed to the living room where three large windows let the daylight in and opened onto a splendid view. Boris was almost moved enough to contemplate the turquoise colors of the lake filtering through the branches of huge oaks planted in the garden of a house below. On the left, the pointed roof of an old turret pierced the foliage of tall bushes and gave the setting a medieval feel. To the right, the property stretched as far as the eye could see, with a rolling terrain and green grass that was as well cut as a golf course. Across the way, a long mountain ridge, like a stone colossus lying on its side, served as the frame for this landscape.

Michael's visualizing technique was certainly incongruous, but it allowed him to etch the locations of his cases into his memory. Before he photographed them with his eyes, he immersed himself in their smells and sounds. As his sense of smell was already highly developed, he trained it every day in anticipation of such circumstances, where he would have to identify, classify and then record all the olfactory molecules that emanated from the crime scenes. Smells are stored in the deep memory; they are the ones that bring back childhood memories, memories of breakfast in the garden of a country house, or moments spent in an attic playing hide-and-seek.

He had turned off the light of his childhood memories, and all that was left was the light of the places where atrocities had been committed.

Boris directed his colleague to the right and walked along an office where four large computer screens made the room look like a control center. Because of his blindfold, Michael couldn't see them, but his olfactory senses detected something. He took a cautious step toward a bar of some sort that ran halfway across the wall at the back of the living room, then arched his back and lowered his head.

"It smells of alcohol. Whiskey?"

Pavlowski detailed a bottle filled with an amber liquid and replied, "Looks like it, yes."

"How many glasses?"

"Only one."

The two policemen made a mental note of the information and Boris was about to continue their merry-go-round, when Michael broke the silence again. "Let me smell the bottle, please."

The lieutenant shook his head a few times, but resigned himself to the request, despite the fact that he was starting to find it more and more ridiculous.

Michael pulled a latex glove from one of his suit pockets and put it on. He grabbed the whiskey bottle, uncorked it carefully and sniffed the smell coming from the neck.

"Scotch. Good stuff. Aged."

Boris looked up. He felt like he was wasting his time with something that could be read right off the label. Yes, it was Scotch, Balblair, twenty-four years old.

His teammate then sniffed the glass and paused, as if he was searching his memory to extract the different scents he had stored. "This glass contained the whiskey, but there are traces of another ethyl smell."

"Crime Scene are on it, we'll have everything in their report." Boris sighed impatiently.

"Let's go on then."

Over the following minutes, the two men explored the kitchen and two other rooms then they entered a space with closed shutters and next to no furniture.

A strong smell of incense saturated Michael's nostrils and he froze, like a hunting dog on the prowl.

"Where are we?" he asked in a low voice, as if he was afraid of waking someone.

"An almost empty room the size of the others," Boris answered, looking absentminded.

"Describe it to me."

"There's hardly anything, a strange carpet in the middle, an incense holder with sticks, a speaker connected to an MP3 player, and a low wooden cabinet with a bell and a hammer on it."

Pavlowski took a step to the side, grabbed the small hammer and rang the bell.

A high-pitched note echoed through the room for a few seconds, and Michael crumpled, as if seized by a searing pain. He screamed and fell heavily to his knees on the thick carpet. Boris rushed over to him, looking worried.

"Are you all right?" he asked.

Michael tore off his blindfold and put his hands over his ears as if the crystalline ringing, despite the echo having faded, continued to twist his eardrums.

He swayed back and forth.

His superior stepped aside, watching him with a puzzled look.

Who had hired this freak?

After a short minute, Michael calmed down and stood up. Without a glance at his teammate, he inspected the carpet, then the bell, and finally the MP3 player. He went through all the tracks and stood up again. "This is a lotus flower carpet," he said, turning to Boris. "This is a meditation room."

Pavlowski stood there for a moment. A few seconds ago, his colleague was writhing in pain for some reason that was still unknown to him, and now he was talking to him as if nothing had happened. Was this also part of his strange farce?

He did not want to let the incident pass. "Are you going to

tell me what happened? Or are you going to pretend that was nothing?"

Michael did not answer immediately and let a long minute go by. It felt like eternity for Boris. "Don't worry," he assured him. "Just a bad memory revived by the sound of the bell."

Suddenly, his eyebrows arched and his eyes widened. He lifted his chin and Boris thought he saw a smile, the authenticity of which he could not verify.

"It smells like Bluestar," said Michael. "Crime Scene must have found something."

In the downstairs bathroom, several techs were working in an eerie silence that didn't bode well. One of them, wearing the same full-body suit as the two policemen, leaped out of the ultraviolet halo cast by the room and, for a moment, the whole scene looked like a remake of a bad science-fiction movie. He quickly climbed the flight of stairs and stood in front of Boris and Michael, who had just come out of the meditation room.

"Blood trails all over the bathroom! Someone tried to cover it up by cleaning it, but it's still fresh."

Captain Assia Jenkins waited for silence in the big room. "Traces of blood were found in Colin Vassard's bathroom," she said solemnly. "They have been sent for analysis. I demand perfect cohesion between the investigation teams and a great speed of action: we don't know if the people on this list are still alive or not. Maybe our suspect has locked them up somewhere, maybe he has one or more accomplices: I want to be informed of everything, and quickly!"

Her tone had not sounded authoritarian; on the contrary, it had fired up the spirits and motivated the troops. Deep down, Emma was pleased that a beautiful mixed-race woman like Assia Jenkins could lead a precinct mostly composed of males with such fervor. She had just arrived, but everyone already respected her, so she didn't need to prove herself anymore.

Emma had just received the videos from the cameras placed outside the small police station in Bloomfield, where the strange man had turned himself in. In the background, in the upper right corner of the image, one could see the emaciated silhouette of the man getting off the bus. The ticket found on him confirmed this version. Apart from that, they had no serious leads.

Suddenly, Jamal became agitated and turned to Emma. "Detective Emma Ann King, I've got some news!" he said, using her full name and rank as per the custom of the precinct. "I've just received all the addresses of the people on the list."

She smiled, and with a good push of her leg, rolled her desk chair toward Alsayed.

"Jenni Grosch-Steiner," he continued, stumbling over the name, "198, Oxford Street, near Park Avenue. Then we have Tod C. Sheepmann living at 64, Greenwood Street, not far from here, and finally, Slevin B. Bradich, 162, Gregory Hill Road."

The young woman moved her face towards the screen and frowned. Every time she did this, a tiny dimple appeared in the center of her left cheek. "Tod with one D and Sheepmann with two Ns?" she asked.

"Yes, weird, but I mean, you saw the guy who wrote that list. A weirdo too."

"Word," she whispered to herself. She stood up, patted Jamal's shoulder and headed to Assia's office to report back.

After she was allowed inside, she scanned the room and thought to herself that Captain Jenkins still hadn't decorated it.

It had been almost two months since she took office, and not a single detail of her personal life had transpired. Nor had she tried to cover the traces left by the multiple photo frames that Henry Saget, her predecessor, had placed all over the room to immortalize the trips he had taken over the years.

The young woman observed her superior for a few seconds, without moving. Assia seemed buried in a thick file whose obvious complexity made her frown, giving her a serious look. Emma noticed that her forehead showed no wrinkles, even with that grimace of concentration, and she found her even more attractive. She was the perfect love child of two continents; continents she would have gladly delved into.

"I'm listening," Assia said, cutting off Emma's train of thought.

"We have the home addresses of all the names on the list."

"Very well," she answered while raising her head. "Split up the research between all the teams and report to me as soon as possible. We'll leave our friend in the *fridge* for a few hours before confronting him with the leads you've found."

"If we find any."

"That goes without saying, Detective."

Jenkins tilted her face and stared at her paperwork again, a sign for Emma that their conversation had just ended. She stole a furtive, mental image of her superior and left the office.

6

Jenni Grosch-Steiner, the second alleged victim on the list, lived in a small apartment in a three-story art deco building. Everything in the area had a post-war feel to it, and if one ignored the few reminders of modern life, one might have thought they were back in time, almost a century ago.

Every time she passed through these old streets, Emma was overcome by a strange sense of nostalgia for a long-ago era she had never known.

Jamal had contacted the Pavlowski-Monroe team, and was informed that Crime Scene were already packing up their gear.

If Emma's fearful, strange feeling was confirmed, the technicians would no doubt be called back and put to work on this new crime scene.

The detective rang the bell several times. No answer. The frail wooden door gave way at the first knock, and the two investigators, guns drawn, quickly found themselves inside the apartment.

A strong smell of patchouli assailed Emma's nostrils, and she briefly considered that Michael would surely have been able to break down every olfactory element. She missed him. Prior to his burnout, she and Mike had been a great team, and their results had been praised by their boss at the time.

Jenni Grosch-Steiner's apartment consisted of a living room with an open kitchenette and two bedrooms. One of the bedrooms had a window that looked out onto the street, the noise of which was barely muffled by the single pane of glass.

A bed with pink satin sheets, heart-shaped pillows, a night table where a bedside lamp rested, and a wardrobe topped with mirrored doors. The room did not reveal any clues at first sight; the Crime Scene techs would be in charge of unveiling its secrets, thanks to DNA and trace evidence.

The second room, on the other hand, plunged the investigators into a very different world, far from the impression of a well-behaved girl that the little they had already inspected seemed to suggest.

A rack on wheels held dozens of sexy outfits: vinyl dresses, latex suits, garter belts, fishnet stockings and other disguises, obviously intended to satisfy any fantasy. The bed was bright red, and its image was reflected in a large mirror mounted on the ceiling. If Emma and Jamal still had any doubts about Jenni, the objects displayed on a white cabinet in plain sight shattered them in an instant. Dildos of various sizes, shapes, and colors were piled up there, seemingly waiting for their happy hour.

Detective Alsayed laughed, but Emma remained impassive. She slowly walked over to the bedside table and reached for a tin with the label of an old brand of tea. When she opened it, everything became crystal clear. "Either she has a very sexually liberated roommate, or our Jenni is an independent escort girl!" she said to her teammate while pointing to the bundle of bills piling up at the bottom of the tin.

Jamal widened his eyes, as if trying to make the embarrassment showing on his face disappear.

The two detectives continued their tour of the apartment

and found the source of the incense smell that saturated the atmosphere. A tiny room, more like a large closet than anything else, was wedged between the toilet and the bathroom, not far from the entry door. Inside, both were intrigued by a lotus flower mat, a bell and a portable speaker.

"What's all this?"

"I have no idea," said Emma.

She bent down and put her hand on the mat.

"Ouch! Damn, that hurts! What the hell is this?" she shouted.

"It looks like a mini fakir mat," he tried.

"Anyway, I don't know who this Jenni 'Thingy-Steiner' person is, but there's something wrong here," she said, standing up again.

"You say that because of her *special* room?" he asked, mimicking quotation marks with his fingers.

"Not even..."

She frowned, giving the feeling that she was thinking deeply before speaking. "There is something wrong, something that bothers me. An intuition..."

"You know what I think about intuition?"

"No, but I know you're going to tell me."

"Intuition is good, but evidence is better. You don't build a case on hunches, let alone a murder charge."

"Let's call Crime Scene, we'll know more after they're here," she added.

While Emma made her call, Jamal quickly continued his search of the premises. On the hallway cabinet, he spotted something that caught his eye.

In a ceramic bowl, a few nickels had been left amongst metal hair clips and a set of keys. The keychain was from a well-known car rental company, and Alsayed was suddenly reminded that he had seen a gray SUV parked in the small parking lot behind the old building. The image of the "Rent A Car" sticker caught his attention too, as he was supposed to arrange for a rental car for his upcoming vacation with his girlfriend. Despite having promised her, he still hadn't done so.

"Detective Emma Ann King," he said as she pocketed up her cell phone, "I think I found her car."

He held up the keychain and shook it like a child's rattle.

Emma approached him and he thought for a moment that she was going to take the keys out of his hands, but she continued on her way to the cabinet in the hall.

She opened the only drawer and searched it. She took out a new bundle of bills – much less substantial than the one in the *special* room – and a black moleskin notebook. Curious, she flipped through it and realized that it was an agenda.

Every Tuesday, the same letter was written, a B.

She scrolled through the pages in search of other clues, but soon found herself at the end of the notebook, where a directory served as a means to store contact information. Under the letter B, a single name, obviously written by the same hand, and a phone number.

***

Boris and Michael had been driving towards Slevin Bradich's home for twenty minutes, and only the voice of the GPS had spoken. The electronic device indicated that the destination address had nine minutes of driving time remaining.

Michael watched the scenery through the car windows and detailed the pedestrians they passed, all dressed in winter jackets on that first day of spring. Boris thought it would be the longest nine minutes of his life, and then, remembering that he had a colleague he had met only a few hours earlier seated next to him, he decided to break the silence, competing with the digital sounds of the satellite navigator.

"How come Jenkins suddenly brought you into this case?" he said. It sounded like an accusation.

He doesn't know yet, thought Michael. He welcomed this and answered without looking away from the road. "I've convinced her that I'd be more useful working on this case than wrapping up old reports."

"Okay," Pavlowski said, scratching his right temple.

He didn't believe him. Michael remained silent.

Boris was definitely stuck with the least talkative cop of the precinct. But he did not despair; everyone always ended up talking to him, Monroe would not be an exception.

"What's your take on this investigation then?" asked the tall blond.

"Not much. We don't have enough to go on yet," Michael replied in a voice so low it barely covered the sound of the engine.

"If you ask me, the suspect is a drug addict with nowhere else to go, who made up this story to draw attention."

"And what do you make of the blood found at Vassard's?"

This time, he had turned to Boris: the subject suddenly seemed important enough.

"You know," the lieutenant replied, "it seems to me that anything is possible these days. Once I had a case where a pool of blood was found in a bathtub and it came from a sheep that had been slaughtered for the feast of Eid."

"There's nothing in Colin Vassard's apartment that indicates he's a Muslim."

"I grant you that. I've never seen such an empty and

impersonal place. I'm just saying that until we get the blood report, we can't know for sure it's human."

Michael's face closed, and he turned his head to watch the landscape unfold before them again.

The road snaked amongst rows of identical buildings whose only visible differences lay in the floral arrangement displayed on the balconies.

In spite of the omnipresence of all these uniform concrete apartment blocks, the decor had nothing resembling a shady city of suburban zones. Greenery was everywhere. Numerous flowering trees saturated the spaces between the road and the houses, and the mountains – eon-old witnesses of immemorial times – offered a majestic background to the picture.

"Your destination will be on the right," said the digital voice of the GPS.

The two cops got out of the vehicle. The doors slammed in unison and Boris hurried to stand in front of his colleague.

"Are you going to do the blindfold trick again?" he asked, looking almost worried.

Michael froze and stared at his superior for a long time. An eternity seemed to pass. "I know it sounds strange, but it helps me to fix the details of each case deep inside. I need to record the smells, the arrangement of objects, the sounds, all those little things that sometimes make a difference."

Pavlowski had never heard him speak in such long sentences before. He paused for a moment and sighed, shrugging his shoulders. After all, he said to himself, there was not much risk that anyone would be there to witness their embarrassing pantomime, and if Crime Scene were to sweep the place, Monroe's circus would already be over.

Without any response from Slevin Bradich, the cops kicked the door down.

Michael adjusted his blindfold and took a deep breath. The place smelled musty, and sometimes, when the two men stirred the air with their movements, subtle hints of oriental spices could be detected behind the pungent smell of the apartment.

Sergeant Pavlowski had placed himself behind his colleague, his two powerful hands resting on his shoulders, and was leading him as if in an unusual game of blind man's buff. "The tour will quickly be over, there is only one room," he said.

"Let's do it anyway."

The tall blond man complied, promising himself that it would be the last time.

They walked along the counter of a kitchenette and Michael slowed down. He bent down slightly and said, "Curry?"

Boris glanced at the sink, which was overflowing with dirty bowls, and opened one of the overhead cabinets. "Packets of Chinese noodles... curry flavor, yes," he admitted. "You'd think that's all this guy eats, there are at least fifty of them."

He inspected the next cupboard and discovered cardboard boxes stacked to the top; condensed milk this time.

The fridge revealed an impressive amount of Red Bull energy drink cans, and painted an obvious portrait of the tenant.

They continued their slow procession and Michael stopped again. "It smells like sweat."

"There's a single mattress at our feet. When you take off your blindfold, you'll get that the sheets weren't changed very often."

Pavlowski's last word echoed through the room, and then silence took over.

Michael turned his head to the left and listened. Something had caught his attention. A discreet, almost inaudible sound that seemed to blend in with the ambient background noise. "Is that the air con?" he asked.

"What?"

"I perceive the light sound of a fan..."

"It must be the computer behind us, I think it's still on."

As in the first missing person's apartment, a computer – consisting of a unit with a faint reddish halo pulsing slowly from it and two screens – was sitting on a desk at the end of the room.

Michael took off his blindfold and walked over to it. He moved the mouse with a brief gesture of his hand, and the electronic machine snapped out of sleep with a quiet hum. The main screen displayed the page of a website neither of the policemen recognized: Twitch.tv. The graphic designs seemed to indicate it was a video host website.

The login and password, saved in the memory, had pre-filled the input fields, and all Michael had to do was click on the connection button.

He entered the user interface and was struck by the sheer number of videos displayed. The account name, "SlevinFortnite", confirmed to the investigators that this was the person they were looking for.

Michael swiped the mouse icon across the page and clicked on one of the videos, which he put on full screen.

Before their eyes, the credits rolled, accompanied by electronic dance music, and then a man appeared. He was wearing large round sunglasses with leather side shields, similar to those traditionally worn by mountaineers. The rest of his face was camouflaged by a black bandana, whose white patterns drew the lower part of a skull.

Slevin Bradich, if it was indeed him behind this disguise, was speaking in front of the camera and presenting the rest of his video. From what they understood, they were going to watch one of his games in the online game Fortnite, where he had set a new record for frags.

After the short introduction, images of the game scrolled by and the video showing Slevin was reduced to a small rectangle in the upper right corner of the screen.

"Techs will take care of the computer sweeping; I'll call Crime Scene and we'll head back to the precinct," said Boris.

Michael was absentmindedly listening and after a few seconds, he turned around. "You didn't tell me there was another room," he said, pointing forward.

"It must be the bathroom or the toilets," replied the tall blond man with an absent look.

Michael opened the door and revealed a tiled room that included a shower, a toilet and a piece of furniture with peeling paint topped with a basin.

The strong smell of incense almost made him recoil, but what he spotted further inside invited him to enter.

Rolled out on the floor, a carpet identical to the one found at Colin Vassard's, and also on the floor, in a corner, a small bell and its hammer.

A few seconds later, Boris followed him.

"The same lotus flower mat!" Michael said. "This bathroom was his meditation room."

Pavlowski pointed to a black plastic object on the edge of the shower tray. "And here's the smart speaker; everything is the same as at Vassard's place," he said, frowning.

Michael scratched his head, looking lost in thought, and Boris wondered if he'd bothered to listen to his last sentence. Working with this weird lonely guy as a partner was going to be more and more complicated. But he had to hold on, let him trust him, and a time would come when he would have total control of the situation. Then it would be the end of these esoteric methods that led nowhere, and he had good hopes of restoring a little order and discipline to a department that had been left to its own devices for too long by the former boss.

Boris watched his partner return to the computer and shook

his head, rolling his eyes at the ridiculousness of the scene: Michael, like a truffle dog, was leaning over the desk and sniffing the objects on it, as if he was going to discover the key to the whole mystery by dissecting olfactory molecules. He lingered on a half-empty soda can near the keyboard and put on a latex glove before grabbing it. He brought it to his nose and then turned to Pavlowski. "The same smell as in the whiskey glass at Vassard's. It's very subtle, but I'm pretty sure it's identical."

"What do you make of it?" asked his teammate, suddenly intrigued despite himself.

"No idea, we'll have to wait for the analysis results."

Your act isn't much use, in short, summarized the lieutenant for himself.

The flow of his thoughts was interrupted by the ringing of his cell phone.

As Michael continued to walk around the studio, he could hear bits of the conversation.

"Very good," said Boris, hanging up the phone, and then he said to Michael, "Something new has come up."

"Emma and Alsayed's team?"

"Yes. They found a phone number in one of the victims' diaries, and they determined who it belonged to. The guy's coming to the station."

"Alleged victims," said Michael.

"What?" said Boris, grimacing.

"The people on this list may still be alive; you're talking about them in the past tense as if you were already sealing their fate."

"Our stranger did say that he had killed them all, didn't he?"

"So he's not a drug addict talking nonsense anymore?"

7

———

Between the two of them, Pablo Almeida and Patrick Fischer weighed over four hundred and fifty pounds; two big babies whose personalities were as different as their bodies were similar. Almeida, the son of a Mexican immigrant, was inclined to good food and excess of all kinds. Fischer, a judo instructor at the local police club, was more into sports and healthy exercise.

Nevertheless, when the duo formed by the two colossi went somewhere, they did not go unnoticed.

Fischer had received a call from Pavlowski asking him to wait for him and Michael before sealing the premises and calling in Crime Scene.

Parked in front of Tod Sheepmann's apartment block, the two cops looked as busy as they could. Almeida had just raided a nearby bakery and was gobbling down buns as if his life depended on it. Fischer, meanwhile, was watching a video on his cell phone, in which a well-built athletic trainer was extolling the virtues of a certain brand of protein supplement.

"Tod Sheepmann? One D, two Ns?" said Almeida as Patrick raised his head and turned to him.

"Yeah, yeah, but apparently that's this guy's name," he replied.

Almeida rinsed his last mouthful with soda and raised his chin toward a car rolling in their direction. "Isn't that Monroe and Pavlowski?"

"Yep," said Fischer, who had shifted slightly to the side to better observe.

"Recess is over," shouted Pablo, then he crumpled the paper bag stained with grease and tossed it onto the floor of his car, at Patrick's feet.

The latter congratulated himself for not having taken his own vehicle to make the trip.

The building overlooked the group of four men with its ten floors, and its façade engulfed by Virginia creepers on all its surfaces gave it a certain charm. The policemen entered the large lobby – whose architecture and basic decor dated from its construction in the 1960s – and they climbed to the third floor.

Inside, the pungent smell of mustiness jumped out at them. It was as if the apartment had not been aired for decades.

Anticipating his teammate's request, Pavlowski faced Michael and took on a serious look. "Michael," he said calmly, "we don't have time for your... for your method. There are four of us, we collect the first evidence, we call Crime Scene and we're out. The clock is ticking and so far, we don't have much."

Michael felt the knot in his stomach again. He was disappointed, he would have inspected the apartment with his eyes closed in order to register all the sounds, all the odors, but Fischer and Almeida, already gloved, searched the rooms like two elephants in a China shop.

The place gave him a feeling of sadness; everything was

empty except the entrance, which hosted a dusty old upright piano, and the room where a yellowed and ageless mattress was placed, askew, without concern for harmony.

All the windows were sealed with aluminum foil, and the only noteworthy detail of the entire place was in the kitchen, where a mountain of cans stood above a greenish-toned tile floor.

Maybe Boris was right after all: there wasn't much to be gained from this search. Perhaps they had indeed better things to do at the precinct.

<hr>

On the way back, the two men did not speak to each other. Pavlowski remained focused on the road while Michael mentally listed the meager evidence they had gleaned. He would need all the help he could get when questioning the strange man, and confronting him with strong evidence would allow him to observe his reactions and lead him to say more. For the moment, the fight was still unbalanced: he had almost nothing.

It was only when they arrived at the police department's parking lot that he deigned to come out of his silence. "I'd like to question our guy, to gauge him, to push him to his limits," Michael declared.

"We'll do that, yes," said Boris, turning back to his colleague while continuing to walk. "Emma told me that you specialized in this."

"Yes, the title is a bit pompous, but I am a synergologist."

Boris raised his eyebrows. "And what does that mean?"

"It's the science of non-verbal language," Michael replied.

"Non-verbal language?" the tall blond man asked.

"Yes, you have to know that communication between two

human beings is not only done with words. Speech represents only ten percent of language."

"And the other ninety percent?"

"Emotions, subconscious phenomena, smells, hormone flows, hand and facial tics: there are thousands of mechanisms that take place in the body of a human being who communicates with another."

"Okay," Pavlowski admitted without expressing astonishment, although deep down he was thinking: *bullshit.*

For this American-born Russian, there was nothing more effective than tangible and indisputable evidence. He abhorred all the pseudo-scientific methods and charlatan tricks. Even with solid evidence, criminals were not convicted often enough for his liking. In his opinion, basing an investigation on far-fetched leads was counterproductive.

When the policemen entered the precinct, the place was bustling with activity, and their colleagues from Groups B and C hardly nodded their heads to greet them. Instinctively, Michael approached Emma. "So, what's up?" he asked.

Focusing on her computer screen, where the content displayed on it seemed to take over her entire being, she finally looked up and, seeing that it was her friend, gave him a big smile.

"Strange case... you?"

"Strange indeed. We have conducted searches at Colin Vassard's, Slevin Bradich's, and Tod Sheepmann's apartments, all of which were nearly empty. There seems to be some connection though: we found a sort of meditation corner in two of them."

She frowned, and a glint shone deep in her eyes. "Tell me more," she enjoined him.

"A special mat, incense, a bell and a device to play music... relaxing, I guess."

The redhead's mouth rounded and her eyes widened. It was as if she had discovered a large package wrapped under the tree on Christmas morning.

"A mat with some kind of pins, right?"

"Yes," said Michael, who, as usual, remained enigmatic.

"You found these at everyone's house?"

"All but Tod Sheepmann's, who had the weirdest place by far. Aluminum foil on all the windows, a stock of cans that would make a survivalist swoon, no electrical appliances..."

Emma tightened her braid in a quick gesture, something she would do a dozen times a day, then she cleared her throat. "What seems strange to me is that we have almost nothing on them in the files," she said. "We don't have much. Their addresses, water and electric bills; but no social security numbers, no cell phone plans; as if they were real ghosts!"

He paused and wrinkled his nose, a sign that he was thinking. "Maybe they're foreigners with a pied-à-terre here in the US. Did you see their names?"

"Yes, that would explain a lot..."

"No internet bills?"

"No, why?"

"At Vassard's there was a big workstation and at Bradich's, a computer set up to play online games. Foreign or not, they had broadband installed at least."

"Not in their name anyway," Emma replied, returning to her screen.

"Hmm... how come they have water and electric bills in their name, but no internet provider?" He had asked the question almost to himself.

Suddenly, the police officers in the open space all straightened up, in a disorderly fashion, and the hubbub stopped. Assia Jenkins had just entered the room, and Michael felt a twinge of sadness again, as if he was rediscovering her every time she appeared.

"I have an update on our case," she said to the audience. "Pavlowski, Alsayed and Fischer, gather your troops and meet me in the briefing room."

Realizing that all the information gleaned by the various investigative teams would have to be cross-referenced, they each gathered personal notes, files and photographs before following their captain.

The meeting room, or *briefing room* as Assia had renamed it, consisted of a set of tables in the center, a large whiteboard with traces of markers that never quite faded, a computer with several screens, as well as an overhead projector and a constantly empty water fountain.

When Michael walked in, many memories of Henry Saget, his former boss, surfaced. He couldn't count the endless hours he had spent here, untangling the threads of complex cases, day and night. A page was turned with the arrival of Assia. His colleagues had had nearly two months to familiarize themselves with her methods; he would have to learn on the spot.

When everyone was seated, Captain Jenkins, standing in front of the board, began her speech. "The Crime Scene techs have just confirmed traces of blood at the homes of all the victims. They had been cleaned up and were revealed by Bluestar. The ones found at Tod Sheepmann's house, however, are much older."

She paused and looked each of the officers in the eye. When it was Michael's turn, she blinked several times and quickly moved on to the person next to him, Boris Pavlowski. *She's embarrassed*, he thought. Her facial tics told him so.

"We have several problems," she said, grabbing a blue felt-tip pen. "First of all, the identity of our guy in custody."

She wrote the word on the board followed by a question mark and continued, "Then, where are the victims?"

She proceeded in the same way and wrote down the four names, each with a question mark as well.

"And finally," she concluded, "when we have all this, we will look at the circumstances of the crimes and their motives. Before we do that, do you have any questions?"

Emma raised her hand and Assia gestured with her chin, giving her permission to speak. "You say the blood found at Sheepmann's is older: do we have an estimate?"

The captain rummaged through a file on the table in front of her, then answered, "The traces are a few months old, between two and six, while those at Grosch-Steiner, Bradich and Vassard are all recent. Between twenty-four and forty-eight hours, according to Crime Scene."

There was silence in the assembly. The case seemed to become more complicated as the police discovered new elements giving everyone the impression of groping along the edge of a precipice in the dark.

"In my opinion," said Assia, breaking the calm, "the most important thing is to find the victims."

She surrounded the list of names with two concentric circles.

"All we have to do now is get our weirdo to talk, so that he can at least tell us what he did with the bodies," said Boris.

His last words seemed to have awakened something in Michael, as if he was stung to the core.

"Maybe he's holding them somewhere, maybe he has one or more accomplices? As long as we don't have any evidence to the contrary, I think we should consider the victims as still alive."

"And what do you do with the blood?" retorted Pavlowski, shifting to his right to face his colleague.

"Maybe he only injured them."

"And his confession? The fact that he keeps telling anyone who will listen that he killed them all?"

Boris had scratched his Adam's apple and lifted his chin. His non-verbal language was a sign of his affirming hierarchical superiority.

"Why would a man turn himself in and confess to a quadruple homicide without giving his identity? I have the feeling that he is afraid of something. Maybe he's under duress, maybe he was forced to take the blame for the murders."

The idea seemed to be gaining ground in the minds of the officers, because no one contradicted Michael.

"Well," said Assia suddenly, "Alsayed, tell us about your search at Jenni Grosch-Steiner's house, and then we'll let Lieutenant Pavlowski take over this meeting."

Jamal ran a hand through his slicked-back hair and stood up. "Detective King and I conducted the search of Jenni Grosch-Steiner's house," he began, without saying the name wrong this time. "We found a lot of cash in the apartment and a room which seems exclusively intended for a paid sexual activity," he continued without being able to dissimulate a giggle of embarrassment. "We'll have to look into home-based prostitution, in my opinion. We also found a rented vehicle whose papers directed us towards an out of state agency. I put colleagues on the case, it will take a little time, but we will have the name under which this rental was registered. Finally – and this is much more concrete – we have the identity of a certain Bruno Costa whose telephone number was written in a book at the victim's home. He'll be here tomorrow morning before going on his shift for work. That's about it."

"And the meditation stuff?" Emma asked.

Alsayed looked confused and frowned. "The mat?" he asked, looking in her direction.

She nodded positively, urging him to go on.

"Oh yes... uh... we also found a mat with hundreds of spikes, a bell, a hammer, incense and a Bluetooth speaker... a kind of relaxation or meditation kit, in short."

"A lotus flower mat!" Almeida said. "My chiropractor told me to use it for my lumbago, it's awesome."

All the faces turned to the imposing policeman, seemingly waiting for an answer.

"What? Maybe she just has a bad back, that's all."

No one replied and the room remained silent for a few seconds. Almeida was a good cop, despite his rough and tumble nature. No one blamed him for the intervention because it could possibly prove useful. The floor was then passed to Boris.

The six-foot-six blond with Slavic features rose up in a fluid and disciplined movement. He quickly readjusted the collar of his shirt and began his speech. "So much to say about the homes of Colin Vassard, Tod Sheepmann, and Slevin Bradich... and so little at the same time."

His voice seemed to drop a few semitones, as if to become more solemn, or more imperious, Michael thought.

"At Vassard's, not much except the now famous mat that was found in a room dedicated to meditation or relaxation. We don't have any data from social services, but considering the high rent of the apartment, we can conclude that he has substantial financial means. Technicians are combing through the computer as we speak. It's password-protected, but that shouldn't take more than twenty-four hours to crack." He swallowed slowly and continued. "Same thing with Bradich: we don't know how he earns his living, but we have a lead. He's a kind of YouTuber specialized in video games, and with the rather large number of views he accumulates on his profile, it's a safe bet that this has become his job. Again, to be confirmed or not with the tech guys. As for the meditation space, elements common to the other three were indeed found in his bathroom. However, at Sheepmann's, everything is quite different: no relaxation space, no electrical or electronic devices, in fact, not much at all. Aluminum foil on the windows, as if he was afraid of magnetic waves: I've seen this before."

Seeing that he didn't seem to want to say anything more, Assia allowed herself a question. "So we have an obvious link between three out of four victims. Maybe Sheepmann's "meditation space" (she mimed quotation marks in the air) is somewhere else and we haven't found it yet. In this case, similarities between all of them would be the practice of this discipline... It's thin, but it's a lead that can't be ruled out."

"Maybe they all go to the same yoga club or some kind of cult," said Almeida.

Cult. The word was out. Michael inwardly flinched and prayed that no one would notice.

Assia suddenly glared at him. He sensed in the micro-expressions on her face that she had meant to say something, but had changed her mind.

He was going to have to deal with this particular problem head on, he knew. He couldn't get away from it, but as if to distract him and give himself an illusory reprieve, he said he wanted to question the strange man and confront him with the evidence they had already gleaned.

"Be my guest, Monroe, be my guest," Assia Jenkins thundered, ending the meeting on the spot.

8

———

The detainee was still lying in the center of the cell in a fetal position. Boris and Michael had brought him something to eat and drink, and once he had eaten his meager meal, they accompanied him to one of the interview rooms.

Just before the two policemen left the meeting, Emma had quickly approached Michael and slipped him a piece of information that seemed to interest him greatly; the man had mentioned "the Captain" which caused him to have a panic attack before sinking.

As usual, Lieutenant Pavlowski made sure that everything was in order before continuing.

Michael sat down in front of the strange man and began to detail him. Despite the dark circles that distorted his thin face, his shoulder-length hair was smooth and he was clean-shaven. The cold of his cell had obviously taken its toll on him, for he was regularly overcome by shivering and yet his forehead was beginning to be slightly beaded with sweat. He remained docile and calm, but he glanced around furtively at the slightest movement or unexpected noise.

Who could this guy be, the guy who accused himself of four murders, without wanting to say more?

Boris started the recording of the interview, and Michael stared at the man for several seconds before asking his first question. "Are you ready to tell us a little more?" he said as the man lowered his head like a dog used to being beaten with a stick. "We checked the names you gave us, and we're starting to believe you. Did you really kill those four people?"

"I killed them all, I killed them all," he whispered, cowering.

Drops of sweat were now falling at a steady pace, staining the desktop. "What should I call you?" said Monroe. "If we're going to talk, I need you to at least tell me your first name. My name is Michael."

The man did not blink, as if the detective's question had been lost in the limbo of his sick brain.

At times, however, a grimace disfigured him and his face remained tense for a few seconds, as if frozen with pain.

Too many external elements were interfering with the deciphering of his non-verbal language and the young synergologist was beginning to lose patience, just like Boris who chose this moment of hesitation to step into the interview. "Colin Vassard, how did you know him? And Jenni Grosch-Steiner?"

The man wasn't listening, he was holding his stomach and gritting his teeth.

"Are you sick or something?" Pavlowski asked coldly. "Did you eat too fast? If you feel like throwing up, you should tell us right away."

The stranger's only answer was a muffled grunt, foaming at the mouth.

The two investigators looked at each other, powerless.

"What's wrong?" Michael asked, suddenly worried, putting a hand forward to grab the man's shoulder.

His shirt was soaked. He withdrew his hand and watched him writhe in pain in his chair, but remained outwardly impassive. The suspect looked to him like an insect struggling on the surface of the water before sinking and drowning. Boris suddenly looked worried; something was definitely wrong.

"Did the Captain send you?" Michael dared to ask him.

The mention of the name seemed to accentuate the torment the man seemed to be undergoing, as if the detective had made an additional turn to the crank of the vice that was compressing his whole being.

Suddenly, he let out a long, bestial scream that bounced off the walls of the room. As if he was being eaten from the inside. He was convulsing more and more, then a last jolt threw him backwards and his chair overturned. The handcuffs that bound his wrists stopped the movement, and he fell to the ground in a position so unnatural that it gave him the appearance of a disarticulated puppet.

Boris and Michael rushed to the strange man, whose tremors redoubled in intensity.

Michael placed a hand on his forehead; he was boiling. "He looks like he has quite a fever," he said to his colleague.

"I'll call paramedics," Boris said, grabbing his cell phone.

The man's stomach clenched again and he vomited the remains of a barely digested meal onto the floor.

Sitting in the uncomfortable chairs of a hospital waiting room, Michael and Boris were killing time in their own way. The tall blond was surfing the web on his cell phone, looking for fishing tackle for his next break, while his partner was finishing his Rubik's cube for the eleventh time now, with a plastic mechanical noise that was beginning to annoy Pavlowski. He had opted for the 4x4x4, bigger and more complex than the original, whose resolution sometimes gave him trouble because of the many exceptions in the solutions that he had to learn by heart.

At the back of the room, two swinging doors opened to reveal a young intern in a pale-green surgical coat, holding a couple of X-rays in one hand and a pen in the other.

The two men put away their toys and stood up together.

"Good afternoon, gentlemen," he said in such a solemn tone that Michael almost thought he was going to give them a military salute. "The patient you brought in was in pretty bad shape. A fever of almost 104 degrees and a full-blown infection."

Boris raised his eyebrows, Michael remained impassive.

"He didn't make it easy for us," he said, "he didn't want to tell us anything. After a few minutes of examination, we found the cause."

The intern took a few steps forward and stood under four neon lights and held up one of the X-rays. The harsh hospital lights filtered through the translucent paper and revealed the secrets of their stranger's insides. Part of his ribcage was visible, and below the sternum, a diffuse, almost spectral mass that must have been his stomach.

At the end of it, one could make out an object whose perfectly cut contours were unmistakable and known to all. Such a thing could never have been there by accident and, as far as the intern could recall, he had never seen this before.

Planted there for an obscure reason in the middle of the viscera of a person without identity: there lay a key. *The key to the mystery?* Michael wondered.

"We proceeded to do an enema and then a quick surgical operation to extract the key," explained the man in green.

"Did you keep it?" Micheal asked.

"Of course," replied the intern. "It has been cleaned and sealed. Hold on, I'll get it back for you from the nurse."

He was about to disappear into the hallway, but turned around. "Uh... you want to keep the X-rays?"

"The key will suffice," Pavlowski said in a peremptory tone.

The doors swung open for a few seconds after he passed, leaving the two policemen in the middle of the waiting room in a moment suspended in time.

No one said a word until the intern returned.

"Here it is," he said, handing them a plastic bag with the object inside.

"Good, thank you. Where is our man now?" Boris wondered.

"He's in the recovery room, still recovering from the general anesthesia."

"Some of our colleagues will come and wait for him to regain consciousness; then he will have to be placed in an isolated room. They will explain everything to you."

"All right," said the aspiring doctor.

"Another thing, how long will it be before he can leave the hospital?"

"Only a few hours, it's like having an appendix operation."

"Okay, thank you very much."

They greeted the intern and headed for the exit.

The smell of ether mixed with industrial detergents brought back bad memories for Michael. He hated hospitals, but as eager as he was to leave this squalid building, he slowed his pace until he stopped dead in his tracks and turned back one last time.

"Please?" he hailed the young man as he was about to enter the ward.

"Yes?"

"You did a blood test, right?"

"Yes, the anesthesiologist ordered one before the operation."

"Anything to report?"

"Nothing. Not exactly what you'd call a healthy person, but nothing alarming."

"No traces of drugs, psychotropic drugs?"

"Nothing of the sort, officer," the intern replied awkwardly.

Michael turned on his heels without thanking him and hurried outside.

In the car, as the two men settled down, he dared to remark, "The junkie thesis no longer holds."

Almost surprised to hear the voice of his colleague, Boris opened his eyes wide. "Junkie or not, what kind of person would swallow a key?"

Michael grabbed the bag and scanned it from every angle through the plastic. "We have to find out what it opens," he whispered.

9

Through the bay window of the precinct, the spectacle was grandiose. Showers had dampened the foliage of the trees, which were trembling in the gusts of wind, and in the distance, the sun was dipping behind a mountain in an uncertain sky, torn between threatening charcoal clouds and an almost clear horizon, whose iridescent colors of twilight gave hope for better days.

If it hadn't been so cold, there is no doubt workers would have gathered in the lakeside bars and restaurants to kick back after a good day's work. But the first day of spring was already closing in an electric and stormy atmosphere that did not bode well. How long would this cold snap last?

The last few hours had been long and full of events that needed to be digested, so Captain Jenkins came to the conclusion that her teams would be more efficient after a good night's sleep. She gave them all an appointment at dawn for the next day, and the police officers said goodbye to each other before dispersing.

Michael, who was not staying in the barracks, walked slowly

to his car, treading on the glistening tar of the parking lot. The petrichor scent instantly took him back to distant memories. Sure, he hadn't had the same childhood as most people, but in the midst of all the turmoil, he had managed to build his own world. Even as a child he loved nature and animals, and whenever he was allowed to go out he had imagined many exciting adventures among the tall grass, moss-covered rocks and young hazel trees.

He unlocked his car with his remote key fob, and the familiar voice that called out to him in the distance behind him almost startled him. His insides knotted up and, before turning around, he looked at the tube of anti-anxiety drugs floating in the ocean of nickel coins in the central pocket of the car, like a bottle at sea.

"You can't avoid me like that forever."

It was Assia.

Her voice was icy. Michael noted, however, that she had been the first to speak.

All day they had treated each other like strangers: he couldn't back down now. "Not here, Assia, not like this in the parking lot," he replied, looking almost sheepish.

"Agreed. Take me out for a drink then."

It sounded like an order. After all, Captain Jenkins was his superior.

He complied and opened the passenger door for her. He walked around and stepped into the vehicle.

The indecipherable gaze of the beautiful African American, caught between anger and pity, scrutinized him in his every move. He fixed on a point of the horizon right in front of him, as if forbidden to any interaction. Michael Monroe in a nutshell, unable to behave like his fellow humans and to express the smallest reaction.

In a deleterious silence, he drove the car along an avenue which skirted the lake, toward a destination still unknown. A big black cloud was now veiling the sky and it had started to rain again. To the hum of the engine was added the intermittent rubbing of the windshield wipers, but still no sound of any voice.

"Here, the Majestic Bar!" Assia suddenly shouted, pointing to a brewery at the corner of a building.

Without saying a word, Michael nodded and entered the adjoining parking lot.

Before getting out of the car, he took one last look at his medication and closed his eyes for a long time. He concentrated on his breathing for a few seconds, then followed Assia who was already running for cover.

There was no worse place for a reunion. It was cold and decorated in those taupe tones so wrongly praised by TV design shows.

A waiter pointed to a corner of the room where a table surrounded by two gray leather benches and too much lighting made it unwelcoming.

"Still no alcohol?" Assia asked as she sat down.

He shook his head.

"I'll have a spritzer, please," she said to the young man.

"And for you, sir?"

"Sparkling water."

She plunged her dark eyes into Michael's. She contemplated his face and saw only suffering and dejection there. The rings under his eyes were hollowed out and, judging by his prominent cheekbones, it seemed to her that he had lost some weight. He was still as pale as ever, and his jet-black hair did not help.

The minutes ticked by like eons. The waiter finally brought them their drinks and Assia took a sip of her cocktail.

"Two months, Mike. Do you realize what two months without any news feels like?"

He clutched his glass so tightly he thought for a moment it would burst. He took a deep breath to try to clear the lump of stress in his throat and replied, "I was not well at all, Assia. Nothing against you..."

"I would have been there for you if you had wanted me to," she said, rolling her eyes. "Not a call, not a text, not even to tell me 'Listen, Assia, I'm not well, I don't want to talk to anyone.' I would have understood that. Silence is the worst, Mike. I even thought you were dead."

"I'm sorry," he huffed. "It's always complicated with me, you know that, you've always known that."

She took a big sip again. She still had a lot to tell him, a lot of anger that had been pent up for months between the walls of her heart, but thanks to the alcohol she was beginning to relax.

"What did I do to deserve that you cut me out of your life, just like that, without notice?"

"It has nothing to do with you, Assia."

"*It's not you, it's me*, right?"

He paused for a moment before answering.

"Kind of, yes. I wasn't feeling well, I didn't want to talk to anyone and I thought of reaching out to you, but you know how it is the longer you wait, the more insurmountable it is. It became a vicious circle."

"Besides, you knew I had taken the new chief position at the Rochester PD. And you disappeared the very day before I arrived. You have to admit that there is something to worry about, don't you think?"

"It's an unfortunate coincidence..."

"I know, I looked at your file, Michael," she said, cutting him off. "I have a feeling that Saget covered for you before he retired, and I'm sure the report I read didn't tell half the story."

"You want to know what really happened? Is that why you brought me here?"

Another gulp of spritzer. The glass was now empty of its orange liquid, only ice cubes and a slice of lemon were dueling inside. She held up the emptied container and gestured to the bartender to make her another one.

She adjusted her posture and the faux leather of the bench squeaked. She looked into Michael's eyes.

"It's crazy how clumsy you can be. I don't care what happened! What I want to know is why you left me without even giving me an explanation."

He suddenly widened his eyes.

"I... I didn't leave you, Assia."

The woman's eyebrows rose, forming two perfect arcs. Her face almost showed amused amazement.

"You've been off the radar for sixty days, I haven't heard a word from you; what do you call that? You're very smart, Michael, so don't make a fool of yourself!"

He took the blow and moistened his dry mouth with a dash of his sparkling water.

"Okay, I messed up," he admitted in a shy whisper. "Talking, opening my heart, expressing my feelings, you know that's not my thing. Emma always says I was raised by wolves."

"That's probably true," Assia said with a smile as her cocktail arrived.

"I've totally lost it, you know. I've had a hard time getting back on track."

He was finally breaking out of his shell, and she detected a naive sincerity in him that moved her. This guy was a real mystery, but she felt deep down that, despite all his flaws and that thick armor, she had before her an ultrasensitive and caring being.

She placed her hand on his in an affectionate gesture that Michael greeted with a tiny, contrite smile.

"If you haven't left me, what do you want then?" she asked in a soft voice.

He inhaled several times and tried to breathe with his stomach as he did during his meditation sessions.

A tear rolled down the corner of his eye. She had never seen him cry.

"What do I want, Assia? I would like to get rid of this pain that gnaws at my insides, of this constant uneasiness that eats away at me when I look at the world with a teary eye, of this sadness that invades my days and destroys my nights when I think of what humanity is at, at the end of the day: a profoundly egotistical species that is playing God and destroying everything in his name. My skies are always gray. But somehow, when I lose myself in your eyes, Assia, I forget all of this."

Michael's words had touched her heart, her pulse was now racing. She knew that such a speech from such a withdrawn person was a rare thing. She etched every word in her mind, especially the last ones.

"That's why you're a cop," she told him calmly, her hand closing over his. "You're here to try to fix this world a little."

"Like a Band-Aid on a wooden leg, yes," he replied cynically.

As a group of young people sat noisily near them, Michael and Assia seemed to have created their own bubble of silence. With their eyes locked on each other's, time stretched.

"Where are we then?" she asked finally.

He thought she was beautiful, there, sitting in front of him. He had always found her attractive, from the moment he had seen her at the back of the classroom, on the first day of his synergology training. He was there to study for a diploma, she was there to report on this new field and to see if it could, in the future, be integrated as a specialty in that of the police force.

Her perfect face seemed to never register the stigma of time, her bright white smile contrasted with her brown skin, and her dark eyes, full of mystery, were like two onyx beads that looked as if they had witnessed the birth of the world.

By her side, he felt vulnerable; and the crazy desire that she would protect him like a small bird fallen from the nest took hold of him at each of their meetings.

There, in that old-fashioned brewery with a decor as cold as the weather outside, Michael relived what he had felt for this woman a few months earlier. He wanted to throw himself into her arms and forget everything: him, what he was, the case, this world...

Assia gave him a charming smile. The two spritzers had made their small effect: her guard was down for now, and she would have liked to jump on him to taste his fleshy lips.

"Come," she whispered in a languorous breath.

She rose and took his hand, leading him towards the exit. He let himself be led without protesting, like a ship adrift saved by the halo of a lighthouse in the open sea, which pierces the night with its providential light.

Back to the barracks, back to the world of the precinct, disciplined and structured. But they had both forgotten their jobs and the case that had kept them busy since the morning. They slipped stealthily into one of the residential buildings reserved for officers and went to Assia's apartment.

A few boxes from her move still littered the floor. A perfect illustration of the life of being a cop, a ghostly being who always seemed to be in transit and who can only give little time to their private life, as if the balance of the world – the one between good and evil – depended entirely on them.

They stripped each other on the way from the front door to the bedroom, making a mess of shirts, pants and underwear.

They made love as if it were the last time. Michael was intoxicated by Assia's scent, a sweet mixture of vanilla and caramel. Even her sweat, slightly musky, inebriated him, and he realized at that very moment that he had missed her body stretching against him.

After the ecstasy, the two naked lovers stayed still a few minutes in the middle of the crumpled and wet sheets of their lovemaking.

She turned over, climbed on Michael to come to lie down on him. He felt her pubis rubbing against his belly and opened his eyes to her beautiful face whose swollen lips looked like two delicious candies.

"You sleeping over?" Assia asked in a suave tone.

Michael made a slight grimace.

"I can't, sorry," he replied, thinking of the horde of felines he fed every morning. "Next time, for sure."

Assia had anticipated his negative answer, but could not hide her disappointment.

He slowly caressed her cheek, plunged his eyes lovingly into her gaze for a few seconds, then gently pushed her away before getting dressed again.

"Mind you, there won't be a next time," she said, "unless we go to your place."

A feeling of panic made him almost shiver. He had never let anybody penetrate his intimacy. But nobody had ever managed to enter his heart as deeply as Assia had done. Surely, there was a beginning to everything.

As Michael remained silent, she continued, "Do you realize

that we've been seeing each other for months and that I've never been to your place?"

"We were meeting in New York..."

"Nevertheless, *you* spent a weekend at my place. You could have offered me the same thing in return."

"Do you remember how the 'weekend' ended?" he said, mimicking quotation marks in the air.

She shrugged. "Fair enough. But at least you saw where I lived back then."

"I have to go," he concluded.

As Michael quietly exited the apartment, Assia pulled the blanket over her and turned on her side in silence.

***

Outside, the thickness of the night made the scenery disturbing. Chilly gusts of wind swept through the fallen leaves on the ground. Michael felt as if he had never been out of this dreary season, and the weather proved him right.

He returned to his car and reached for his anti-anxiety medication. He swallowed a pill which, with nothing to drink, scraped his esophagus with pain.

He drove for about twenty minutes through the deserted streets that the darkness had taken over. Here and there, however, streetlamps pierced the blackness with their gloomy light. The anti-anxiety chemicals finally did their job and he relaxed. His pupils dilated and he felt a strong urge to make a detour before heading home.

He loved the night and it was returning the favor.

A mournful mist rose over the lake and dispersed into the townships on its outskirts. He thought that the elements were with him, that they were hiding him under their vaporous and benevolent veil so that he could move in the shadows as he pleased, without fear of being seen, of being judged.

In a business park a few blocks from downtown, Michael stopped his vehicle behind an industrial-looking building whose charcoal façade was illuminated by a red neon sign. Its fluorescent letters read: Gravity Zero.

From the poorly lit alley where he had just parked his car, one could hear the infra-bass coming from the club that Michael was heading towards.

A metal door barred the entrance, and after the peephole slid open to reveal two green eyes topped with huge fake eyelashes, it opened without delay.

The female gaze actually belonged to a tall black man who greeted Michael. His muscular arms protruded from a long red dress with spangles, and his wig, of the same color, gave him a contradictory appearance between a basketball player and a cabaret dancer.

"Well, dear, it's been a long time!" he said jovially in his deep voice.

As the cop remained silent, the tall transvestite continued, "Participating or just peeping?"

In response, Michael grabbed one of the masks on the counter and stepped behind a heavy black velvet curtain.

The music was deafening and the lights were pulsing; he had to slow down to accommodate the visual and acoustic aggression. His olfactory senses were also taken by assault. The mixed scents of mentholated electronic cigarettes, alcohol, latex, rubber, candle wax, and lubricant were fighting in his nostrils.

Creatures of the night brushed against him, half-man, half-woman, subs on leashes walking on all fours, tattooed and pierced bodies in the most unlikely places. All were there to satisfy their most unavowable fantasies, to indulge in practices that their own society saw with a bad eye. There, though, nobody could care less, everybody was free and consenting.

He took a deep breath and finally soaked up the atmosphere. He hadn't been there since his leave, and judging by the feeling of bliss that was overwhelming him, he definitely missed that club.

Guided only by his memory of the place, his body seemed to move like a robot, passing through two corridors to a padded door. Michael opened it and slipped into the room.

The lighting was minimal and he had trouble distinguishing if anyone was already inside.

He reached forward and pulled back a large curtain to reveal a rectangular window that opened into a new space. A one-way mirror – the same size as the one used back at the station – separated him from the spectacle on the other side.

An older man, his hands and feet shackled with chains, was being penetrated by a slender, athletic young woman with a strap-on dildo, while someone whose gender was impossible to define because of the full-body latex suit they were wearing, was whipping his genitals with a leather horse whip.

But Michael wasn't there for that. After a few minutes of this unorthodox show, a languid shiver ran through his body when he felt a warm breath on his neck. "You are back, at last," said an androgynous voice.

As in a Pavlovian reflex, he completely undressed at once, keeping only his mask which had guaranteed his anonymity for so many years, then he lay down on the ground.

The creature of the third sex, with long, sleek black hair and a bust belted in a red vinyl corset, began to gently stomp on Michael's back. The dizzying heels of her platform pumps, the same blood-red color as her lingerie, sank into Michael's skin, crushing muscles and ligaments, pinching nerves and twisting flesh.

The pain helped him to connect with a world he did not understand anymore and, in the cries of suffering which he repressed with great efforts, he found some answers to his questions.

10

———

Bruno Costa had kept his word. He showed up at the Rochester police station that morning for an interview. He was offered a cup of coffee while waiting for Boris and Michael to be ready to hear him, but he had declined the offer.

He was a shy little man with brown hair as greasy as the skin on his face. He was withdrawn and seemed to want to curl up into an invisible shell whenever he was spoken to. Uncomfortable in his seat, he fidgeted constantly, while trying to be as discreet as possible. To avoid having to turn his head and observe his surroundings, he rolled his eyes from right to left to their maximum, like a sick chameleon.

When Boris's deep voice called his name, Bruno almost jumped. "Mr. Costa?" he repeated, standing in front of him. "Will you come with us, please?"

Sweat was already beading on his forehead as he followed the two officers to one of the interrogation rooms.

Michael held out a hand to show him a chair and motioned for him to take a seat.

Mouth slumped, eyelids slightly drawn upward by arched eyebrows: Costa was scared. And judging by the amount of cheap perfume he had sprayed on his body before coming, he had a sickly fear of death.

Michael kept his eyes on the man's hands and face, looking for any other signs that could be analyzed. This guy was an open book.

When his full name was mentioned, he surreptitiously scratched his left earlobe, an unconscious sign that it was indeed him the policemen were talking about.

Boris glanced at his notes and began. "Does the name Jenni Grosch-Steiner mean anything to you, Mr. Costa?"

"No, it doesn't," he answered in a shy voice.

His pupils had just dilated rapidly and he had put his hands under the desk. It was obvious to the synergologist that he was lying.

"Are you sure you don't know her? Maybe not by this exact name. Do you know anyone called Jenni?"

At this new mention of the name, Bruno rubbed his philtrum, the small gully of skin between the nose and the lips. "No, I don't know any Jenni," he replied, peremptorily.

Boris stirred in his chair and sighed before continuing. "Mr. Costa, we are in possession of certain elements that suggest that you know a certain Jenni Grosch-Steiner."

Once again, the little man slid his index finger over his philtrum, and scraped the base. There was no doubt about it now: there was something sexual between him and the girl. If, as they all thought in the precinct, Jenni was a prostitute, the link between them was quickly made.

Bruno had also repeatedly swung his face to the left side, staring blankly at the ground. This guy was expressing shame without realizing it.

Michael was able to quickly establish his emotional and relational portrait, which allowed him to take the lead in the interview. "Mr. Costa," he said in a calm, caring voice, "I'm going to play it straight with you. We have strong reasons to believe that something serious has happened to Jenni. We don't know where she is, and we're trying to do everything we can to find her. I don't care what she does for a living or what you did with her."

He paused to observe the effects of his words. The features of the man's face were slowly beginning to relax, and his hands loosened: he was gradually trusting the policemen.

"If you're sleeping with Jenni for money, that's not our problem, that's not why you're here; we think you might have information vital to our investigation."

Another silence, then Michael resumed, "You're Jenni's client, aren't you, Mr. Costa?"

Bruno filled his lungs and raised his head. "Yes," he answered in a soft voice. "But it's not what you think, we don't... well... it's not sexual."

"GFE?" said Detective Monroe, voluntarily using the jargon in the online prostitution sites.

"Yes, that's it."

Without knowing it, Bruno Costa had just given them a new element that Michael hastened to exploit. "What website?"

"What website?"

"You found Jenni on an escort website, didn't you?" said Michael, raising his voice.

The man wiped his glistening forehead. "Uh... yes."

"So, give us the address, please."

Costa pretended to search his memory to find a website he had been visiting several times a week for years. "Uh... escort-models.com."

Boris scribbled the name on a notebook and spoke up in turn. "And you can find Jenni on this website?"

"Yes," said Bruno, lowering his gaze.

"When was the last time you saw Jenni?"

"Last Tuesday."

Michael thought back to the day planner that was found at the girl's house, the letter B written on the page for every Tuesday. All of Bruno's body language proved to him that he was telling the truth, but Michael detected subtle glances to his left, his eyelids a little slack. Something was wrong.

He and Boris worked Bruno Costa over for nearly two long hours. He gave them most of the important information for their investigation at the beginning of the interview, and as time went on, the information became more and more trivial.

In the end, they had not learned much more. Nothing that would allow them to find Jenni Grosch-Steiner dead or alive. Bruno had admitted that she was a prostitute and that he went to her house every Tuesday. She apparently never went to her clients' homes and he himself did not know any others. Sometimes they dined together at the pizza joint around the corner; the employees would surely confirm that fact.

After releasing their man, Pavlowski and Monroe joined the teeming mass of the open space to blend in. Emma, with a word-puzzle magazine in hand, approached them with a smile. "Anything new?"

"Not much," said Boris, "but we have something worth checking out."

The tall blond man moved to his workstation and opened the internet browser. Michael addressed the young woman. "You? Got something new or just having fun with your word puzzles?" he called out, unusually sarcastic.

"Come on!" she growled in a friendly tone. "I don't give you shit when you play with your Rubik's cube every five minutes! And for your information, we're making progress. We're having a breakfast briefing in the lounge later, you'll see."

He nodded and walked over to Boris's desk, his computer

screen was now displaying the website indicated by Jenni Grosch-Steiner's client.

Ads for dating sites with questionable wordplay polluted both sides of the browser window, and in the center, dozens of photos of half-naked girls were competing in this salacious digital marketplace.

Each of them had a personal file where their measurements were mentioned, the terms of the appointments – at home or at a hotel – a short welcome text that was directly addressed to the future client and, finally, the price per half hour. No ambiguity there.

On the header of the site, Boris spotted clickable keywords that made it possible to sort out the different profiles. The men who used the services of this new kind of prostitution obviously didn't have much time to lose in this sex supermarket. They needed it done and quickly. One could choose according to sexual practices, breast size, skin color: a real detailed catalog.

Checkboxes followed by city names were located in an insert at the top right. Boris clicked on Rochester, and the page refreshed. The number of results dropped drastically. This time, only about fifteen girls were available. This gave an idea of the extent of supply and demand in their quiet little city.

The photos, each more suggestive than the last, scrolled before the stunned eyes of the three cops, but there wasn't the slightest trace of Jenni Grosch-Steiner.

Pavlowski started again, more slowly this time, and scanned every profile, read every word, but nothing matched the little they knew about the missing prostitute. "We don't even have an idea of what she looks like," he grumbled. "For all I know, she could be one of these fifteen girls and we wouldn't even know."

"There are email addresses and phone numbers on every profile," Emma suddenly said. "What do we do, put a team on it and contact them all, pretending to be clients?"

As if the stars had aligned at that very moment, Pablo Almeida moved his heavy frame behind the group and made a smutty comment. "Are you shopping for tonight?" he said.

"Good timing, Almeida," said Boris, turning around. "You and Fischer are going to call back the guy we interviewed earlier and see if he recognizes one of the girls as Jenni Grosch-Steiner. In the meantime, first contact all the escort girls and ask to be received at their home. If the girl we are looking for has removed her profile from the website, perhaps the other girls know her or have heard of her."

The detective's eyes widened and he seemed to suppress a chuckle. "All right," said Pablo.

As their imposing colleague recorded the website address, Michael's face darkened. "Costa didn't tell us everything," he muttered.

"How so? Because we can't find her?" asked Pavlowski. "Maybe the murderer took it upon himself to erase the traces of his victim's escorting activities."

"That's possible, but I'm sure he's hiding something. His head kept tilting to the left, his hands were clenched under the table and his toes were planted in the floor. He tried to minimize it, but it was stronger than him. He's afraid or ashamed of something."

"Using an online prostitution website is already shameful enough, don't you think, Michael?"

"I'm not making any value judgments," he replied calmly, "I just know that he didn't tell us everything..."

"You're the expert in these cases, aren't you? You didn't manage to make him crack?" Emma said, accompanying her reply with a wink.

He moved abruptly away under the perplexed glance of his two colleagues. They saw him seize a plastic bag on his desk and return slowly towards them. "Let's leave that aside for the moment. We have much more urgent matters."

He put down the key that had briefly been in the strange man's stomach.

"We must know what it opens," he thundered. "At all costs!"

11

———

Alone at his desk, Michael felt the tentacles of anguish creeping through his body, like a deadly poison flowing through all his vital organs. He closed his eyes and let his thoughts take over. A cloud of geometric images assailed him; they were all similar: those of the logo printed on the rectangle of cardboard paper that the stranger carried in his pocket. A triangle and the letter G, printed in an ink as black as the memories evoked by this evil sign.

Despite the fact that Michael had freshly returned to the precinct, Assia had agreed to include him in the investigation because of this important detail, this symbol that represented a cult he knew well. If the stranger had anything to do with it, they shouldn't waste time and follow the lead. But Michael was putting off revealing this information to Boris. He knew that his colleague would force their team to go there and, after everything Michael had been through in the last two months, he was not ready to go through such an ordeal again.

The thought of his anti-anxiety medication came back to him, and he was glad he had left it in his car. He breathed in slowly and focused on the fresh air flowing in and out naturally, without having to act on it. The oxygen that filled his lungs connected him with the world around him. This simple breathing movement was an allegory of the struggle he had been going through all his life: fighting to make himself belong to the world of the living, the world of men and women.

He had never known why he felt more akin to the animal kingdom than to his fellow humans. He had totally hidden this detail in his weekly sessions with his psychiatrist, for fear that she would detect in him a lack of empathy that would bring him closer to the serial killers he was supposed to go after. According to him, nature was perfect and mankind was its degenerate son, the glitch in the system, the grain of sand in this well-oiled machinery. He thought he had chosen this job for this reason – perhaps unconsciously – in order to repair this Darwinian anomaly that was humanity. The cops undoubtedly thought they were making the world a better place; but he, Michael Monroe, wasn't satisfied.

The chaotic flow of his reflections was suddenly interrupted by the familiar voice of Assia, whose glance he had hardly acknowledged, in spite of their night spent together. "I'll see you all at the briefing, but first, please make a detour to the break room. Breakfast is on me!"

A few laughs and remarks of satisfaction burst out in the assembly, then the human mass left the open space.

The break room had been left in the same state as the day before. The buffet on the tables at the back of the room and the "Welcome back" banner was still waiting for someone to notice them. The case that had shaken up the station for twenty-four hours mobilized the entire contingent, and no one had had any time to set foot back in this room. Assia had arrived at dawn, at the same time as the employees of the cleaning company, and had expressly given the order to leave everything as it was. A fleeting glance at the slogan welcoming Michael back reminded her of her lover from the night before. She felt a twinge of guilt and, at the time, she had wondered what could be wrong with this guy. But there were more urgent matters, and in the thick fog of the investigation they were all in, there was unfortunately no place for sentimental thoughts.

The cops pounced on the food like a herd of hungry hyenas on a fresh body, minus the screams and bad smell. Michael spotted the appetizers suitable for his diet and headed for the buffet as well. The lump in his stomach still made him feel uncomfortable, so he pretended to eat with an appetite, just to please Emma, who had been kind enough to think of him by providing vegan food.

Alsayed raised his voice above the din. "The test results came in this morning!" he said. "I'll let you finish your breakfast and tell you about it right afterwards."

Michael turned to Emma and shrugged inquisitively. She approached him with a glass of apple juice in her hand. "We've got a lot of stuff, a lot of new leads to follow. Too many, if you ask me. This investigation is going in all directions, no way to see clearly."

"Crime Scene techs made any progress?" he asked in his familiar neutral tone.

"Eat something first. I'll see you in the briefing room right after. And drink something sweet, you're all pale!"

After a quick snack, all the cops involved in the John Doe case – the "list" case, as they had dubbed it among themselves – met in the adjoining room. Pablo Almeida had brought in some groceries, which he placed in the center of one of the tables. "Help yourself if you're still hungry," he said good-naturedly.

When everyone was seated, Emma took a few steps to face the assembly, in the same place as their boss the day before.

Michael looked around and saw that Assia was not present.

"Well," said the redhead, "there's a lot to talk about and I'd really like your full attention. Jamal and I have prepared a little summary file, which we'll email you all; but before that, here are the things we know."

She walked over to the whiteboard and added her handwriting to that of her boss. "First of all, Colin Vassard. The search of his computer and internet browsing history tells us that he is probably a trader. And a pretty good one, considering the amount of money he earns every month. He has several accounts with different brokers, and all the money he makes is wired to a bank account with an English IBAN. So far, it doesn't match anything in our database, but we're digging into it. His apartment seems to belong to a real estate company established in Panama called CTRE – but here again, the financial set-up is complex. Many legal entities hold shares left and right, but at the moment, no legal person. No names. Surprisingly, it's the same real estate company that owns the apartments of all the missing people on the list..."

Reactions of astonishment broke the relative silence left at the end of her sentence, then the calm returned quickly.

"We located a vehicle in the parking lot of Jenni Grosch-Steiner's building," Emma continued, "whose keys were inside her home. The SUV was rented from a company by the name of CAV Trading. It doesn't take a genius to make the connection with our trader: Colin A. Vassard."

"That's because you do word puzzles all day!" said Almeida to lighten the mood.

The remark was greeted by the young woman with a smirk and a few laughs broke out in the audience. She let the moment pass before resuming. "If we are to believe Bruno Costa's statement, Jenni Grosch-Steiner was an online prostitute. Was Vassard a client? More than possible. Was he the one who hurt her at her place? Did he bring her to his house to finish the job? If so, why would he abandon his car in the parking lot? We're going to have to try and establish a timeline of events if we want to get through this."

She grabbed the glass of juice she had brought, took a sip to clear her throat, and concluded her speech. "As for Slevin Bradich, he presumably makes his living as a podcaster about a popular online game called Fortnite. Again, the income is substantial: he is in the top ten of America's best; he's got millions of views and the tens of thousands of dollars that go with them. All the money made is wired to an account registered in Ireland and, guess what, the IBAN does not correspond to anything known to our services either."

Michael scratched his temple and then intervened. "Do we have the video rushes? They must be on his hard drive, right?"

Emma could see what her friend was getting at. "Hundreds of hours, yes, spread over several hard drives and, guess what? Not once did Bradich have his mask and glasses off. He wore his disguise constantly."

Michael shook his head. "Results of the analysis of the whiskey glass at Vassard's?"

"Hold your horses, I was getting there!" she said in a slightly louder voice. "Traces of GHB, microdosed."

"Which means?"

"Which means that the quantity is not sufficient to be used as a rape drug."

Boris Pavlowski suddenly decided to intervene. "What about these 'meditation corners'?" he said, mimicking quotation marks with his fingers.

"Nothing special, except that all the missing persons use the same objects. The MP3 player at Vassard's only shows a few audio files that, when analyzed, are just white noise."

Michael straightened up in his chair and craned his neck forward, like an animal scenting danger. "Can we listen to those tracks?" he asked.

"Uh... yeah. I can ask for a copy."

She lowered her head and turned the pages of her file. "Sheepmann now. He's the one who gave us the most trouble, but Detective Alsayed had a nose for it. After a simple internet search, his name came up on a few sites. He is credited as a composer on a number of classical music works. I gave it a listen: not my thing."

A few laughs burst out and she continued, "So, we got our hands on the man's royalty statements from the ASCAP. It's not Taylor Swift's, but it's worth a few hundred dollars a month."

"That explains the decoration of his apartment," said Almeida.

Michael instantly recalled the yellowed mattress, the sad and empty rooms, and the pile of cans that littered the kitchen floor.

The young woman paused and looked around at her audience for a question, but the room remained silent. "All right then, gentlemen, that's all we have for now: the next twenty-four hours are going to be critical!"

<hr>

Michael felt as if the morning briefing had done nothing but plunge the investigators deeper into the fog. He was frantically fiddling with his Rubik's cube when Boris approached his desk, looking determined. He pushed aside a stack of files and placed his butt on the desk. This athlete with military and disciplined features was now towering over him with his full body, in yet another dominating posture. "Did you really smell GHB in the whisky glass?" he asked in a doubtful tone.

Michael put down his toy, two sides of which were already finished, and sighed. "My olfactory sense is not as sensitive as a dog's, which can be a hundred thousand times stronger than a human's, but I've trained it a lot. I did detect an ethyl smell that was different from the usual whiskey smell, that's all. It could very well have been part of the actual process of making this liquor."

"But it was GHB…"

"The lab tests beat my faculties hands down, I swear," Michael replied with a feigned smile.

"You seem to be one step ahead of all the other investigators, including me; but since you don't talk much, I wouldn't mind if you shared your thoughts with me."

He was not sure if Boris had just given him a compliment or if it was just an order, so he put on his most serious look and readjusted his chair before speaking. "Honestly, I don't think I'm one step ahead of you. I'm hanging on to details that I'm struggling with."

"Go on," said Boris, leaning in as if to hear him better.

"I'm wondering if our stranger wasn't a victim after all. Maybe he had a connection with the other four, something went wrong and he's the only one left."

"He did say that he killed them all. Why would he turn himself in and appear to be a murderer?"

"He's afraid, he's completely out of touch. Maybe he's been forced to come forward as the culprit, or maybe he's just running away from something, or someone, and he feels safe here, surrounded by cops."

"And why doesn't he reveal his identity to us?"

"For the same reasons. He protects himself by hiding as much as possible about himself. This key that he swallowed is also a way to bury what he knows about this case. If we find what it opens, we'll have taken a big step forward."

Pavlowski scratched the top of his head and winced. "And this connection between the victims you're talking about, what are you thinking?" He had asked the question as if he already knew the answer.

"The only two connections I can think of are the meditation accessories and the fact that all the missing people on the list have the same landlord."

"And that they are, more or less, ghosts. Their names appear almost nowhere outside of this list."

Suddenly, something seemed to light up in Michael's mind. What could justify such anonymity? Protection? Protection against what?

He jumped to his feet. "We have to find out about the real estate company that owns the apartments! That's when we'll know who we're fighting against."

"What do you mean?" his teammate retorted with a frown.

"Who do you think could organize such a thing and accommodate four people, maybe five if our stranger is in the group?"

Boris stood up and widened his eyes. "What? CIA? The army?"

"If we look hard enough and come up against a wall or worse, classified information, we'll know for sure."

Boris remained silent for a few seconds, then looked down at the business card in the center of the desk. "I have another idea," he said, pointing an accusing finger at the cardboard rectangle. "I want us to follow this lead first. You know this logo, right? You know what it means?"

Michael felt the icy coldness of fatality wash over him. He couldn't lie to his superior or obstruct a criminal investigation. He swallowed several times with difficulty and resigned himself to speaking frankly. "The G stands for Gaïa. A cult named The Children of Gaïa," he murmured.

If Boris had felt any surprise, Michael did not see it. His colleague's face remained impassive, as if he already knew the answer to the question he had just asked. "And where is this cult? Here, in this city?"

A lump of anxiety tightened Michael's throat. He had to let a few seconds pass before opening his mouth again. "A few minutes from the police station, by car."

Pavlowski moved to his office, glanced through the glass windows and, noticing the icy drizzle freezing the cars in the parking lot, he grabbed the jacket that was on the back of his chair and headed for the exit. "We're going on a little trip," he said in his deep voice.

Then, as Michael seemed as frozen as a statue, he turned to him and added, louder, "Right away, Michael!"

Pandora's box was suddenly wide open.

12

The temperature had dropped again since the day before and, along the road, columns of smoke rose from the chimneys of some houses, adding their cottony wisps to the grayness of a sky blocked by threatening anthracite clouds. In the car, the heater was set to maximum. Boris was driving faster than usual, and as their destination drew closer, Michael seemed to sink into his seat, a sharp pain ravaging his gut. His superior had used his authority, and he had to comply on the spot. No time for him to go to his car to recover his painkillers. The more he thought about them, the more the anxiety was tangible.

"Can you give me an overview of this particular cult?" asked Pavlowski, breaking the relative silence. "Looks like there's a traffic jam, we'll have time to talk about it."

"It's not the cult strictly speaking," he mumbled while clenching his teeth.

"Something wrong?" Boris asked, turning his head towards Michael, his face looking worried.

"I don't feel very well, but I'll be fine: a temporary panic attack."

Michael looked away, closed his eyes and thought about his Rubik's cube. He mentally studied it and evaluated the different options for completing it with as few moves as possible. His pulse slowed a little and his breathing became more spaced out.

"The Children of Gaïa is the cult," he resumed, "but now, we're going to a sort of branch of theirs. It's located on the same property, but a little further away. The logo on the card that our stranger had is of one of their support groups."

Boris waited a few seconds for Michael to continue, but realizing that Michael was finished, he asked him again. "Go on."

Michael opened the window and took several breaths. The cold air outside did him good. "The triangle with the G in the middle is an addiction center. A kind of AA group, if you will. The cult uses it as a vanguard recruitment post. If you show up and seek support, everything is free and taken care of. Then the weakest minds end up at The Children of Gaïa."

"Our stranger may have gone to them, I told you he was a junkie."

"Maybe," Michael said, struggling.

The lieutenant's face darkened.

"You sure you'll be okay?"

"Just drive... we'll see when we get there."

Pavlowski still had a thousand questions for his partner, but he chose to leave him alone. It seemed that his mentioning of the cult brought back painful memories, and the closer they got to their destination, the paler his face was looking.

They drove away from the main road along the lake and into a sort of green tunnel of trees that seemed to bend down to greet the car as it passed by. Dead leaves swirled from a pile on the side of the road, and the two policemen drove deeper into the countryside on a path that wound through the meadows. As they passed the first fence – where two wooden pillars, both etched with the letter G, protruded from the muddy ground – Michael felt nauseous. His throat tightened, his heart pounded in his temples and ominous jolts stirred in his stomach.

Boris slowed the black Ford down as he approached a gatehouse, next to which a barrier screened the comings and goings of visitors. A young man came to the car and Pavlowski rolled down his window. "Hello," the lieutenant said, "we're from the Rochester PD, we'd like to speak with the person in charge."

He held up the business card found on their suspect. The guard made a ball with his hands and blew some hot air onto his fingers before speaking. "It's the building on your right; park in front of it, I'll call someone," he said.

Boris was almost astonished at the courtesy with which they had just been received but had not noticed how badly Michael was now feeling. Large drops of cold sweat were beading on his forehead and his jaw muscles were contracting frantically, as if to suppress a deathly gasp.

As the car pulled into the parking lot in front of the wooden building, Michael stuck his head out and vomited onto the gravel.

Lieutenant Pavlowski reached into the glove compartment and pulled out a packet of tissues. His teammate closed his eyelids as a sign of thanks and leaned his head out again, waiting for a new jolt that never came.

A few moments later, a woman with gray hair pulled into a messy bun emerged from the house. She was wearing a long wool sweater and a pair of worn-out pants. At first glance, Boris couldn't tell her age. Her almost angelic face looked as sweet as a teenager's, while her clothes made her look older by at least a decade.

Michael glanced at her and slammed the door shut, terror filling up his eyes.

The woman smiled and crossed her arms.

"I... I can't, Boris... I'm sorry, go on without me," Michael stammered breathlessly.

Pavlowski clenched his jaws and grunted before getting out of the car and walking towards the woman.

Michael buried his face in his hands. His panting breath and the pounding of the blood flow in his skull prevented him from hearing their conversation. He spread his fingers and saw his superior handing out his badge, then the business card that had brought them there. There were nods and contrite smiles. The woman did not uncross her arms, a sign that Boris's speech had no effect on her. It was a one-way conversation, as it always had been the case with these people, and with religious people in general, Michael thought. How do you make someone who believes in a higher entity, in redemption after death, in an invisible hand responsible for everything, hear anything? If he had been in Boris's shoes, he would have spat in her face. His tolerance stopped where the dogmas of monotheistic cults began. Despite watered-down speeches of brotherhood between all humans, the believers could not deny their feeling of superiority towards the non-believers. There had always been those who held the truth and those who remained blind, and these two categories of people didn't live in harmony, he was convinced of this – he had the scars to prove it.

The woman suddenly shook her head and retreated to her den, backwards, like a still-hungry black widow.

The gravel crunched under Pavlowski's footsteps as he walked back to the car, looking irritated.

"They only want to talk to you!" he bellowed, the door barely open.

Michael imagined having to go inside that cursed place and communicate with the cult members, and the sensation felt like a dagger slowly entering his flesh.

"No way!" he shouted.

"You look fine now. At least you found the strength to contradict an order."

"Are you ordering me to go inside and talk to them?" he asked, frowning.

Boris saw red. He sighed loudly and then stuck his head deeper into the car. "Look, Michael, this is a criminal investigation with four potential victims, and no one has time for your mood swings. If you're not up to the job, I'm going to ask Jenkins to take you off the case immediately."

He reached into his jacket and pulled out his cell phone.

Michael's blood was boiling, his acuity was suddenly gone. There was no way to decipher the tall blond man's face, no way to know if he was bluffing or not. He stretched out his hand to stop him. "Wait," he whispered in a calmer tone.

Boris lowered his cell phone and stared straight into his eyes, seemingly awaiting an explanation.

His colleague met his gaze, but remained speechless, so he decided to break the silence. "I don't understand why Jenkins put you on my team, you're clearly not the man for the job!"

Michael bit his cheek and focused on the pain that now radiated from his mouth. The coppery taste of blood quickly saturated his buds and he closed his eyelids.

The only reason Assia had deigned to put him on the case was because he was the only one who could enter the ranks of The Children of Gaïa. If she found out that he hadn't even been able to get out of the car, he was in for endless shrink sessions and a leave without pay.

The wound had reopened and, painful as it was, he could no longer back out. His instinct reminded him that he was the only person who could solve this embroilment.

He did some quick breathing exercises in front of an

impatient Boris and collected himself. "Okay. Just give me a minute. Do you have any water?"

Pavlowski leaned over and dipped his arm behind the driver's seat. He held up a flask and handed it to him. "I can't guarantee you that it's fresh, but it's water."

"Don't worry about it."

He drank a few sips and then stared at the empty space in front of him through the windshield. He tried to calm his mind by accepting all the parasitic thoughts that assailed him and letting them drift away like clouds carried by the wind. When the mist cleared a little, he resigned himself. "Let's go," he grumbled as he pushed open the car door.

The slight drop in blood pressure caused by his sudden standing forced him to cling to his partner's shoulder. He shook his head at the demons swirling around him and walked slowly toward the entrance of the house.

When the woman opened the door, he clenched his fists so tightly that his knuckles turned white. She smiled broadly at him. He didn't know her, but she obviously knew who he was. "Follow me into the big hall," she invited them in a clerical voice, "we'll be more comfortable to talk, and that way you can see where our sessions are going on."

She opened a double door with round handles and pushed. A huge room unfolded in front of them and, from the ceiling, a shaft of light illuminated its center in a wide beam. Dozens of chairs, arranged in a circle around the halo illuminating the place, welcomed new or old addicts coming every week to tell their sad stories or spread the Good Word.

As if in a pre-scripted scene, the woman in the gray sweater sat down and spread her arms, enjoining her guests to imitate her. Boris took a seat and, against his better judgment, Michael did the same.

With a jerk of his chin, he signaled to his colleague to begin.

He felt that he had fulfilled his part of the contract by helping them to penetrate the devil's den without a warrant, and preferred to let him speak.

"Miss," said Boris without taking his eyes off Michael, "the case we're investigating right now is partly about this man." He drew out a photograph of the stranger in custody and gave it to her. "Do you know him?"

She searched one of her pockets and took out a pair of glasses with a broken temple. She scanned the fine and angular features of the man in the picture through the dirty lenses. "Yes, of course," she declared straight away. "He came here a few times."

The two policemen exchanged a brief glance. For the first time in the last twenty-four hours, in the midst of their slow progress through the darkness, a point of light flickered in the distance. Was it a mirage? A trap?

"Do you know his name? Do you have an address where we can reach him?" Boris asked in a voice that was almost too soft, as if he were holding a very fragile object that sound could destroy.

"Everyone is anonymous here, it's a sacred rule," she replied immediately.

Michael had watched her every move, even the almost imperceptible ones on her face, and he was sure she was telling the truth.

Their beacon in the night went out immediately.

Pavlowski did not admit defeat yet. "Do you remember anything, any detail that could put us on the right track? The vehicle in which he came here? Was he alone? Who was he talking to?"

The woman shook her head.

"I don't know anything about that, and even if I did, I just explained that I wouldn't betray the trust of one of our guests."

"Miss," he retorted, hardening his tone, "with all due respect, this is a criminal investigation. You are not held to professional confidentiality, and even if you were, I just have to lift a finger and you can find yourself booked at our station for at least twenty-four hours."

She frowned and angry lines formed at the corners of her eyes. In the gloom of this huge hall, this woman now looked disturbing. The roles were reversed when she stood up with a sharp movement, as if offended.

"You are not welcome here!" she hissed like a snake spitting its venom. "Our rules are not yours!" Her eyebrows suddenly unfurrowed and a strange smile formed at the corner of her mouth. "It's my turn to ask questions now," she continued. "Do you know these people?"

Her last words echoed in the room and, in the background, a door that the two cops had not noticed slowly opened, letting out yellow light.

A man and a woman appeared in the glare.

When Michael met their eyes, his pupils dilated and he felt as if he had fallen from several stories high. His heart was plunging into the void, racing as if to fight its way out of the inevitable fate that awaited him.

With bloodshot eyes, he leaped to his feet, grabbed the back of his chair and threw it across the room towards the couple in the distance who were standing hand in hand, like two petrified ghosts. Their host ducked and Boris, totally shocked, just froze.

Michael let out a beastly scream that seemed to shake the walls. No sooner had the echo of his cry faded than he was already running for the exit.

Pavlowski's blood ran cold as he tried to catch up with his colleague. He was unsuccessful. When he sprang out of the building, he saw him on the ground, on his knees, vomiting his guts up once again on the wet pavement.

Watching him curled up over the gravel, the lieutenant was miles away from comprehending the true reasons for his colleague's affliction.

At the end of this dark and gloomy hall, Michael had just seen his parents.

The further the SUV drove away from The Children of Gaïa's compound, the more the pain that was tearing at Michael's insides diminished. He was breathing more easily, his pulse was returning to normal and his mind was slowly coming out of the fog in which he had been immersed for the past few hours.

As for Boris, he was ranting, his hands clenched on the steering wheel. His driving was aggressive and his passenger was being tossed from left to right at every turn. He gritted his teeth and hadn't dared to say a word since the incident. But the silence of Michael was beginning to eat away at him from the inside and, after a few minutes, he cracked. "Dare to explain?" he said in a surprisingly serene voice.

The calm before the storm, Michael thought.

Before speaking, he moistened his parched throat with a swig of water from Boris's flask. The liquid tasted metallic, like blood. "It's complicated... this kind of place, these people... I can't stand it."

"I noticed, thank you. What were you thinking? You ruined the only tangible lead we had!"

"The woman knew nothing."

"Again with your mentalist crap?!"

Michael had never seen him get so angry, but he remembered that he had only known this guy for two days. He'd seen people who hid their true self a lot longer than that. "She didn't know anything," he repeated in a whisper almost to himself.

The road rolled out under their wheels and he stared at a point in the distance, in the void. Under his hoodie, his T-shirt was soaked with sweat, and he was starting to shiver with cold.

"Because of your actions, the doors are now closed to us," Boris said. "We can only go back with a warrant. But that will be too late. I can't do anything else but report the incident."

"Do what you have to do," said Michael with a shrug.

At the top of a hill, the road finally flattened out and Pavlowski accelerated even more. The straight line stretched far ahead of them, and he often looked away from the road to glare at his passenger. The latter ignored him, more out of nonchalance than defiance.

"That's why you got laid off, right?" Boris asked. "You went crazy for some reason and..."

"It's red!" Michael said, cutting him off.

He slammed his foot on the brake pedal and the wheels of the Ford screeched. A split second later, the SUV shook. The car behind had just hit them.

The lieutenant jumped out of the car and called out to the distracted driver. "Can't you open your eyes?"

"You just slammed on the brakes!" the man shouted.

"You have to keep a proper distance, we have safety rules for a reason! Besides, the light was red!"

The tall blond man crouched down to inspect the damage, and the tension went down a notch. The car behind him had just slammed its bumper into the ball hitch of the big Ford.

There was no damage on his side. As for the other car, its grille was a little deformed, but nothing too bad.

For a moment, Michael considered joining in the altercation, but he changed his mind and simply watched from a distance.

"How do we do that?" the driver asked.

"What do you mean, how do we do that? We don't do anything," Boris replied in a much calmer tone. "You're at fault, my car is fine; I'm sorry about yours, but you'll have to deal with your insurance."

"Are you serious? You were driving at a good speed and you slammed on the freaking brakes!"

"You'll have to deal with it, sir," said Pavlowski as he walked to the front of his car.

"We definitely don't have the same way of seeing things!"

"What do you mean?"

"I'm Canadian!"

Annoyed, Boris turned and held up his badge, pulling his jacket slightly apart so the man could see the holster that held his gun. "Listen, I think you've come to the wrong place. Here, it's the USA and I'm the law!"

The face of the Canadian paled and he took a step back. He glanced one last time at his deformed bumper and shrugged in disappointment. Under Boris's inquisitive gaze, he sat silently behind his wheel. There was no doubt in the cop's mind that the driver would soon curse the US Police.

The light turned green and the lieutenant put the car in drive; he then noticed that Michael had changed his attitude. He was no longer slumped in his seat as he had been before the incident, but was sitting upright, and he seemed to be in deep thought. "I may have a lead to follow," Michael said. "Let's go back to the station."

Boris opened his mouth to ask a question, but his teammate had already pulled out his cell phone. "Hello, this is Detective

Monroe with the Rochester Police Department; we brought you a patient late yesterday afternoon and... Ah! Okay, fine, thank you."

Silence filled the SUV for a few seconds, then Michael spoke again. "Yes, hello, this is Detective Monroe, we met yesterday... Yes... Okay... So when will he be back on his feet? Okay, thanks." He hung up and turned to his colleague. "We'll get our man back this afternoon," he declared, his eyes lighting up.

The anger Pavlowski had stored up after his teammate's outburst earlier had dissipated somewhat. He was now certain that Michael would not give any answers to his questions and he decided to play along. However, there was no question of forgetting the loss of a major lead. No, he would make him pay for that later. He was like a mountain lake in the middle of summer, calm and serene; he knew how to break out as violently as ocean waves in the middle of a storm if he had to. His recent transfer to the Rochester PD forced him to remain in the position of a spectator, and every day he struggled to find his real place in the department; but when the time came, everyone would see the true face of Lieutenant Pavlowski.

***

Michael had this annoying habit of speaking only half-heartedly, of expressing his thoughts only as a last resort, as if he feared that if he opened his mouth, his insights would fly away and disappear forever.

With Boris on his heels, he hurried into the open space of the precinct, pushing the two swinging doors open like a cowboy entering a saloon. He rushed to Jamal and interrupted his conversation with Emma. "Did you send our suspect's fingerprints over to the Bureau?"

She replied instead of her colleague. "There you are! I've called you at least twenty times all morning!"

"I was busy," Michael said, sweeping the air with a wave of his hand.

"You look like hell, pal."

Michael ignored the remark and leaned over to Alsayed, repeating his request.

"Yes, of course," said Jamal.

"And?"

"And nothing. Not a hit in the fifty states."

Michael banged his fist on the desk. He then went over to Boris and found him, in front of his computer, busy typing on his keyboard. "Our man seems to be a real ghost, not a single trace of him all over the country. What if he was Canadian?"

"You'll have to send his fingerprints to the country's authorities," Pavlowski replied.

"How long for the results? A week?"

"At least, it's an international warrant: that kind of thing usually takes a while."

"No way! If we don't have anything more on our guy, the DA will ask for his release in a few hours," Michael growled through his teeth.

"That's why we need to get moving and find something ASAP!" Boris replied.

Michael leaned over his colleague's desk, looking almost menacing. "Don't you think I already know that? We have no body, no victim. No victim, no crime! And if he lawyers-up, his pseudo-confession won't work anymore."

Deep down, the lieutenant could admit that his teammate was right; but there was a procedure to follow, and in his opinion, it was impulsive and impatient elements like Michael that were bogging down investigations like the one they were plunged into. A request to the Canadian authorities for a fingerprint match would take a week at best, and it was true that if there was no evidence, the DA's office would terminate their John Doe's custody the next morning. But, given the potential seriousness of the facts, the strange man would be placed under police surveillance and, if the Rochester cops did their job properly, a simple tailing would reveal his home. In the end, if his fingerprints came up somewhere, their man would be immediately picked up and brought back to the precinct.

Michael did not have the same understanding of the system. For him, a suspect on the loose was a threat to law and order and a wide-open door to possible repeat offenses, something he could not accept. He had heard of too many stories – and lived through some – where the guilty took advantage of the slow wheels of justice.

Emma, who kept listening in on what her colleagues were saying, stood up and walked in their direction. "I may have the solution to our little problem," she intervened. "I have an ex-girlfriend who's a cop in Niagara Falls, and we're still getting along great."

Boris's eyes widened. He had just understood in the same sentence his colleague's sexual orientation and that the hopes of doing anything with her vanished at that very moment.

Michael tried to smile and put his hand on his friend's shoulder. "Do you think you can get the fingerprints to her so she can run them through their system?"

Pavlowski jumped up from his chair and stood tall over the young woman. "What about the procedure?" he growled.

"We still request an official fingerprint check," his partner intervened. "But in the meantime, Emma uses her connections and gives us a little help."

"We risk suspension for that, or worse. And if a lawyer comes snooping around, we'll all be stuck with it."

Emma used her soft voice, the one only her lovers would

hear, and only under the sheets. "Lieutenant Pavlowski, I'm just asking a favor from an acquaintance. If anyone is going to be suspended, it's her. Sometimes you have to force fate a little."

Boris sighed and considered what she had just said. Was he going to play the bird of ill omen by reporting this practice and have the whole precinct on his back? It was still too early to take a stand; he was close to the goal, nothing good would come out of cracking now. He would have plenty of time to establish his authority in the future.

"King, Monroe," he said, pointing his index fingers towards each of his colleagues, "nobody saw nor heard anything, understood? Come back to me if you have news; if not, I do not want to hear any more about this."

The young woman smiled and Michael nodded. They finally walked away, their conversation escaping Pavlowski as the distance grew.

He returned to his PC and made sure no one was watching before launching the search engine. He typed in "Michael Monroe" and a dozen newspaper articles appeared.

Let's see what we've got here, he thought.

14

All the detectives had moved into an interrogation room and gathered around the only table. On the tabletop, in the center, was the key that the stranger had ingested, still protected by the plastic of the evidence bag. For the second time in a few minutes, Pablo Almeida picked it up and placed it in front of his eyes, turning it around like a diamond dealer inspecting a new gem.

The metal object did not look like a modern key, but rather seemed to be from the last century, at least. Its structure was peculiar, and one could distinguish a small plate that the patina of time had mostly erased. However, with the help of a magnifying glass, a tiny portion of the inscription was still visible.

Emma and Patrick agreed that the design represented a coat of arms. Almeida had no opinion, and Michael and Jamal thought it was a date or some kind of serial number.

"Stop fiddling with that!" Emma snapped, snatching the key from Pablo's hands.

"I wonder how that guy swallowed this," he said, almost to himself.

She looked stunned. "You, of all people, are wondering how he could have swallowed that key?"

A few sniggers were heard and she immediately regretted the remark; but when Almeida, after a slight pause, started to explode with a big laugh while tapping his large stomach, she relaxed.

"The question is: why did he swallow that key?" intervened Alsayed.

Michael scratched his temple. "He must have thought there was no better place to hide it," he replied. "Which means someone was looking for it. But what does it open? That's the question."

"An old door, a pretty heavy one if you imagine the lock that goes with it," Emma says.

"It's not much, but it's a lead: we can ignore safes and other doors with modern locks," he added.

"Let's publish an ad: 'found old key, make offer'," said Almeida.

The assembly was laughing out loud, except for Michael who seemed to have caught the beginning of a tangible lead in his colleague's joke. "Pablo has something," he said, surprising everyone, including the joker. "I remember a lawyer who used social networks to post a photo of a cap that he absolutely wanted to find out what sort of container it closed in order to exonerate his client."

"And it worked?" asked Almeida, suddenly concerned by the case.

"Yes, the post was shared thousands of times and someone finally recognized the object."

"What do you suggest?" asked Emma.

"The Rochester PD's Twitter account has more than 200,000 followers: I'm sure that a well-worded post with a detailed photo could bring us the solution."

"It will also bring us the media," said Jamal.

"Collateral damage," concluded Michael.

***

Pavlowski was waiting in Assia's office when she returned with a small heater.

"I'm sorry, but I had to get this! The heating system still isn't on in spite of my demands and, frankly, it's too cold here," declared the captain.

"I know them big shots up there: they put off your remarks by counting on the return of warm weather soon. If that's the case, they will have saved money."

"I think you're totally right." She chuckled. "It's crazy to think that it's spring! Every time I look outside, it feels like eternal fall."

"It won't last, and then we'll complain that it's too hot."

Assia paused, admiring the stoicism of her lieutenant. She straightened up in her seat. "You wanted to see me?" she resumed.

He let a few seconds pass before answering. He realized that he was detailing the features of his superior's face for the first time since his transfer. Usually not attracted to women of color, he had to admit it: Assia Jenkins had this *je ne sais quoi* that, with time, had made its way through his mind and made her undeniably charming. Was this sudden attraction to her due to his fortuitous discovery of Emma's homosexuality? In any case, the fact that his chances with her had vanished in an instant undoubtedly gave more weight to the seductive power of the only other woman in the department.

Boris cleared his throat and leaned forward toward the desk. "For the purposes of the case we're on, I need access to precinct archives."

Assia frowned. "You already have it, if I'm not mistaken?"

"It so happens that some of the reports are classified Level 2, and only you can authorize me to consult them."

She turned her head to her computer screen and moved the mouse. "I confess I didn't know that such practices were used here; you know, I arrived only a few days before you," she continued with a smile, without taking her eyes off the pixels.

The bluish reflections of the monitor created dancing shadows on her pensive face. She turned her head in the direction of her interlocutor, her black eyebrows still forming the shape of a V. "Do you think any of the files in our archives could have something to do with the case at hand?"

"Exactly, Captain. Our strange man seems to be connected to a cult called The Children of Gaïa, and it seems that your predecessor, Captain Saget, had some of the reports about it classified at the highest level of confidentiality."

This was the second time someone had come to her with this cult story. First, her lover, who had used his childhood with The Children of Gaïa as an argument to be included in the investigation, and now Pavlowski, who sensed strange maneuvers on the part of Henry Saget.

Assia knew that her predecessor and Michael were intimately linked – in what way, she didn't know precisely – but if the lieutenant could help her get to the bottom of this and make progress on the case at the same time, she had no problem lifting the seal of secrecy. In a few clicks, she granted him access to the files.

"Done!" she said with a smile.

Boris grinned back, and as he left his seat and walked out of the office, a knot of impatience formed in his stomach. He couldn't wait to find out what the former Rochester PD's boss was trying to hide from the rest of his contingent.

Since quitting smoking, Emma had turned her usual cigarette breaks into brain breaks (as she called them), and good luck to anyone who dared ask her anything while she had her nose buried in her word-puzzle book. Her preference was for anagrams, which allowed her to kick back for a few minutes, even in the middle of the noisy open space. Back in the day, her smoke break was six minutes long – she had timed it – so she allowed herself six minutes of that new ritual.

The timer app on her phone played a short melody, and the next second her cell phone vibrated. Nelly, her ex-girlfriend from Niagara Falls, had just texted her. Emma's face lit up and she ran to Michael's workstation.

"Bingo!" she thundered, startling her colleague. "The fingerprints gave us a hit in the Canadian directory: our stranger won't be a stranger for much longer!"

Michael dropped his Rubik's cube and stood up in turn. A slow shiver ran down his spine.

"She's emailing me a scan of everything she has," she continued.

Eager to warn his teammate, Michael called out to him across the large office space. "Boris! Our trick paid off!"

"Speaking of paying," Emma said, "I owe her dinner for the favor. It would be nice if you could pitch in; touristy places like Niagara Falls aren't cheap!"

Ten minutes later, Boris, Michael, and Jamal had gathered around Emma's computer, forming a compact human barrier that seemed to encircle her for protection. She opened her email inbox, clicked on the latest one and displayed all the attachments. In front of the detectives' studious faces, the identity of the man who had been giving the whole precinct such a hard time for more than twenty-four hours was finally revealed.

15

Christopher Tremblay.

The stranger now had a name. And an age too: thirty. As well as a criminal record, since he had received a three-year sentence, five years earlier.

"Bingo!" Emma exclaimed again. She moved her mouse over the next attachment and clicked. "What did you do to get three years in the slammer?" she whispered to herself.

Stabbing in a street in Hamilton, Ontario, three slightly injured, one seriously. The three-year sentence was not actual prison time, but instead a compulsory internment in a psychiatric institution with an annual re-evaluation.

Boris, who had been hovering over Emma's computer, stood up and ran a hand through his blond hair. "Everyone to their workstations! We're looking for everything we have on this Christopher Tremblay here in the US! Emma, go through the file and find the hospital where he stayed, and email the picture of our man to the different institutions in the area."

She turned and frowned. "We've already done that, there's nothing on the psychiatric side... at least here in the US."

"So, we dig further and find everything we can on

Christopher Tremblay on this side of the border," Pavlowski repeated.

He and Michael hurried back to their respective desks. The legal time for custody was melting like snow in the sun; they had to act as quickly as possible.

A relative silence fell over the open space, broken at times by the muffled clicking of people typing on keyboards. While the detectives assigned to "the list" case were busy tracking down Christopher Tremblay, Boris was a lone wolf. Like a hunted animal, he kept glancing around to make sure that the information on his screen did not betray his true agenda.

The tall blond man was browsing through the various minutes and investigation reports archived in the Rochester PD's electronic memory. He used the series of keywords "Children of Gaia" to sort through the ocean of files that flooded his monitor. His mouse cursor turned into an hourglass, and the little icon rotated several times. After a few seconds of waiting, the result appeared: only one file matched his request. And it was filed by Captain Henry Saget.

Each step he took brought back a little pain to his abdomen. The few milliliters of morphine he had been given hours earlier had long since worn off. He didn't know it yet, but keeping silent wouldn't help. From now on, he was no longer the unknown person that wrote "the list", but Christopher Tremblay by his real name.

Two policemen had gone to his hospital room, handcuffed him and asked him to follow them. As the three men emerged from the old concrete building, the cold slapped them in the face and an unpleasant drizzle fell on them, thousands of tiny drops stabbing them like microscopic daggers.

At Rochester PD, Michael and Emma were the ones who welcomed the suspect. They escorted him out of the van and into the bullpen. Christopher Tremblay was back in the *fridge*.

"Welcome home," said Michael as he locked the door.

The prisoner's eyes widened and his pupils dilated. His mouth twisted and a bestial scream erupted from his throat. A blood-curdling scream. A scream of terror. He threw himself forward onto the heavy metal door and began to pound on it. The walls of the hallway shook from the noise, and the two detectives looked at each other, their faces worried.

Christopher Tremblay was shouting the same sentence over and over. "Put me in jail! I killed them all!"

Michael slid the peephole open. The small metal plate creaked and revealed part of the captive's face. His eyes were bloodshot and sweat was dripping down his forehead. The detective stared at him, and the screaming stopped immediately as he shouted back, "Christopher Tremblay!"

The man took a step back, watching his interlocutor intently. At first he seemed shocked to hear his name, then a sneer grew at the corner of his mouth.

As the two cops looked on in amazement, he spun around and crouched down, sticking so close to the walls at the left corner of the room that he seemed to sink into them as if they were made of dough.

Michael glanced quickly at Emma, who shrugged in response. Just as he was about to close the peephole, he heard Christopher whispering over and over like a mantra.

He strained to listen and finally understood.

"Not the captain, not the captain..."

When Christopher Tremblay had arrived at the precinct, Pavlowski had ordered Detective Monroe and Detective King to transfer him to the cell. That monopolized the attention of nearly all the cops, which left him free to consult Captain Saget's minutes without the risk of being disturbed by prying eyes.

The document dated from 1998, more than twenty years ago. Boris knew he had been lucky, because if it had been a few years before, the archives would not have been digitized, and it was a safe bet that he would never have been able to find this report.

Henry Saget had upgraded the file to Level 2 confidentiality, thus removing it from Boris's knowledge; but his maneuvering with Jenkins had just paid off, and the file would give him answers to his questions in a few seconds.

His pulse quickened like that of a child fearing being caught with his hand in the cookie jar. His eyes scanned the screen frantically from left to right, and he had to reread certain paragraphs several times.

The minutes basically described a major search operation in the heart of The Children of Gaïa estate, where he and Michael had gone to get information about Christopher Tremblay a few hours earlier. The intervention followed months of investigation into the alleged fraudulent activities of the cult.

The estate had failed to declare several foreign bank accounts for decades, thus concealing colossal profits. Thousands of accounting documents and all the computers in the various offices were seized, and more than twenty people were brought in for questioning.

From what Boris understood, it was the cult's obscure financial dealings that allowed the tax authorities to file a complaint and refer the matter to the police for a search of the cult's place of business.

The rest of the file contained hundreds of pages of reports of the interviewees. Pavlowski looked at his watch and glanced around. Emma and Michael's desks remained vacant and the officers in the open space seemed focused on their work. He estimated that he had only a few minutes before he would be disturbed. Since he could not possibly read all the interviews, he decided to go through the list of members of The Children of Gaïa who had been screened by the Rochester PD.

One name in particular caught his attention, and he understood at that moment why Captain Henry Saget had prevented anyone without the necessary accreditation from consulting this file.

Twenty-one years earlier, on that very day of 1998, a certain Mary Monroe was interviewed by the police officers. Mary Monroe, née Saget.

16

————

Lieutenant Pavlowski turned off his computer screen when he saw the shadow of his colleague approaching his desk. Michael walked slowly toward his superior, his face devoid of any visible expression. "Our man is in the *fridge*, and Emma gave me the address of the hospital where he was previously committed. We only have a few hours before the end of legal custody: shall we go there?"

His question had the tone of an order, and that annoyed Boris, who didn't appreciate being told what to do by a cop under his command. But since his transfer, he had learned to hide his true nature and to be conciliatory. "Where is it?" he asked without looking up.

"Ontario, near Buffalo but on the other side of the border. About an hour from here."

The answer seemed to embarrass him and he frowned. Michael read his face like an open book. The synergologist sighed and sat down in a chair next to him. "This is the only tangible lead we have," he said in a soft voice.

Boris swiveled in his chair to face him. "It's the only lead we've got left," he grumbled.

Michael let a few seconds of silence pass before resuming. "You think I fucked up our meeting with The Children of Gaïa, but I assure you it's completely different this time. We've got our guy's name and we know where he's from; we're about to make a big move in the investigation. All we have to do is go to Canada, ask around and, if we get a whiff of something, we'll get all the paperwork in order."

Boris shook his head.

"This is a hospital, a public place, we can get in and out without raising any eyebrows," Michael continued.

His superior closed his eyes for a moment and considered the situation. He himself had many questions about his colleague, and he figured that a car trip would be a good opportunity to ask them. "Just you and me then. And we're taking your car," he said with sudden resignation.

The rain had stopped, but the sky remained black and threatening. The thermometer showed temperatures so low that the two policemen had to give in to the protective warmth of their winter jackets. As gusts of wind blew away a small pile of fallen leaves in front of Michael's car, he wondered if summer would ever come.

For the first ten minutes on the drive to Canada, the teammates remained silent. One was focused on the road and the other was consulting his smartphone, looking for answers on social media about that mysterious key.

The picture had been posted a few hours earlier and, after reading dozens of comments insulting law enforcement, useless clues and totally irrelevant monologues, Boris locked his screen and pocketed his phone. He turned his head to the left, looked at Michael for a few seconds and gave him a subtle smile: he was now ready to talk to him. "Mary Monroe," he dropped out of the blue, "does that mean anything to you?"

Michael's hands suddenly tightened on the steering wheel, and he felt his heart jump out of his chest. He was surprised that he hadn't driven them both into the ditch. He reached inside himself to give his answer with the most neutral tone possible. "That's my mom."

Boris already knew that, but he needed more. "What is her relationship with The Children of Gaïa?" he asked.

"She's been a member of the cult for years," Michael admitted.

"Is that why Jenkins assigned you to my team?"

Michael turned the car right at a traffic light, then drove along the lake. A shower hit the windshield and Michael flipped on the wipers. As if fascinated by the throbbing rhythm of the wipers chasing away the rain, he remained silent for a long moment. "My parents joined The Children of Gaïa more than thirty years ago," he replied, clearing his throat. "And the couple you saw when I... well, when I lost it earlier, that was them."

Pavlowski was shocked, but showed no sign of it. He gave him space to continue, but, as he thought, his partner took refuge in his usual silence. "More than thirty years, you say; and you, where were you all this time?"

He looked away from the road for a fraction of a second to stare at him. "I spent my childhood and part of my adolescence within the cult."

The tall blond man thought of a pertinent question that would not risk putting his colleague on edge. He had begun the discussion in a rather cold way and, now that Michael was confiding in him, it was a question of getting him to continue letting him speak his mind without fear. "And this... um... cult, what's its goal?"

"The same as all the others: get rich on the backs of gullible people."

"What does it promise in exchange?"

"The rapprochement between Man and God. You have to strip yourself of all your material possessions and commune with nature to be closer to the Creator. That kind of bullshit."

"And you…"

"I have great respect for nature," he said, cutting him off. "But I'm not a believer and I think this cult is dangerous. I've been away from The Children of Gaïa for twenty years, and I would never oppose their destruction if that was ever a problem for you."

Boris shook his head. "I don't have a problem with the fact that you've been around that cult in spite of yourself. I just like to know who I'm working with. This case is clearly related to The Children of Gaïa, so it's only fair that I ask around."

"I told you everything I know," Michael said.

"Noted," he replied, but he really thought *I don't think so.*

For a moment, he thought of evoking Michael's mother's maiden name, Saget, and the fact that it was the same as that of the former boss of the Rochester precinct. He would have liked to know if it was a mere coincidence or if the truth was much more complex than it seemed. When he thought of Michael's outburst during their visit to The Children of Gaïa estate, he decided to postpone the discussion.

Pavlowski reached out, tuned the car radio to a twenty-four-hour news station, and turned up the volume until it covered the hum of the engine.

His partner exhaled with relief, the interview was over.

The landscape paraded before the car windows, the grayness giving way to more grayness. In the distance, the mountains tore the horizon with their jagged peaks and hilly pastures, looking duller under the monotonous sky. They chased one another for miles before giving way to the urban setting of the city.

At the entrance to Fort Erie, the Saint-Jean psychiatric unit stood above a grassy knoll. From the road, the field showed two distinct shades of green – one, on the left, emerald and bright, and the other, on the right, tending to brown – which blended like two layers of paint on an artist's palette.

The building was imposing in size, but also in its stern, old-fashioned look. Michael wondered how most psychiatric hospitals gave off that gloomy, stressful feeling that he felt was counterproductive to the principles of wellness and healing for the frail people who were locked up inside.

As their car approached, the two policemen realized that the woods surrounding the facility were in fact the grounds of the estate, and it therefore extended far beyond the simple gravel driveway that stretched in front of them and along the front of the building.

At the entrance, an automated wrought-iron gate barred their way. On the left side, a small guardhouse made of old gray stone housed a young man, who seemed much more absorbed in what was happening on the screen above his head than the activity outside.

Michael honked twice and the young security guard was startled, so he put on a peaked cap, similar to the one used by the Marine Police, and went out to meet the two investigators.

"Visiting hours are over, gentlemen: you'll have to come back tomorrow, I'm sorry," he said as Michael rolled down the window to hear him.

The latter then pulled his badge out of the inside pocket of his jacket and held it up a few inches from the doorman's face.

"We're with the Rochester PD, New York State, we're here to see the director," he declared in a peremptory tone.

"Uh... the director, you say?" stammered the visibly impressed guard.

"Exactly. We've come a long way, so if we could keep it short before we leave, that would be nice."

"For sure, right away."

The gate suddenly swung open to let the car through, and they drove slowly towards the hospital's entrance.

The gravel of the driveway crunched under the car's tires, and before Michael closed the window, a familiar, woodsy smell wafted into the compartment. Brief memories of his childhood came back in flashes. He saw himself almost naked, in the middle of a forest at nightfall, lying in the moss in a fetal position to try to keep the little heat his body produced. This ritual had to be done once a week. They fasted all day and slept out in the open in the simplest of clothes: only the children were allowed to keep their underwear on. It was a way for the members of the cult to pay homage to nature, and therefore to God.

He shook his head to make these thoughts disappear. Not that they were bad memories per se, because if there was one thing he had loved, it was the close contact with nature. Everything else revolving around those moments was a pure nightmare.

"You all right?" Boris asked, breaking the silence.

"Yes, don't worry," Michael answered softly.

Lieutenant Pavlowski frowned and got out of the car. He looked up to admire the sculptures on either side of the pediment: small stone angels that seemed to be watching the main entrance.

At the reception desk, on the left, a young Asian woman –

whose almond-shaped eyes were hidden behind an extravagant pair of glasses – greeted them.

"Hello, gentlemen, what can I do for you? Visits are unfortunately…"

"We're not here for that," Michael said, cutting her off. "We're here to see the director."

The receptionist remained silent for a few moments and Boris took the opportunity to slip into the conversation. "We're US Police," he said, slamming his badge on the glass counter.

The young woman didn't bat an eye and simply picked up the phone in front of her. After a few seconds of silence, she got someone on the line. "Mrs. Cooper, there are two policemen who wish to see you."

She hung up. "The director will be there in a few seconds, if you'll wait."

She readjusted her glasses and looked down at her desk, ignoring the two cops.

Michael turned around, hoping to find a place to sit, but saw that the lobby was devoid of any furniture besides the counter.

A few feet down a hallway led to an automatic sliding glass door, the only fragile, translucent barrier separating the world of the sane from the world of the psychiatric patients.

Barely a minute later, Mrs. Cooper appeared before the two policemen. She was wearing a black suit skirt and a puffy shirt which matched the bright white of her smile with perfect teeth. Her thin, symmetrical face, highlighted by very discreet makeup, made her look younger than her position suggested, but her ebony eyes and long, straight, brown hair restored the balance by giving her a severe look. Although beauty is a subjective concept, Michael found her lovely and elegant, and he figured few men could claim indifference to her. Starting with Boris, who was the first to extend his hand toward her, and whose slight genuflection indicated that he was submitting to her authority.

"Follow me," she said in a neutral tone that did not bode well.

The director's heels clicked on the tiled floor of the many corridors they walked down to her office. On several occasions, she had to unlock doors with a key card.

Michael drowned his gaze in all that sanitized whiteness that reminded him of his sessions with his shrink. He had originally imagined a cozy office with warm decor and a comfortable couch, but his weekly appointments were at the Rochester Hospital, in their psychiatric ward. Here, the smell was the same, inducing an unpleasant feeling of unease, of loss of control over his life.

The procession reached Mrs. Cooper's office and she presented two chairs to the two Americans. She waited until they were seated before sitting down in a large black leather chair that looked modern and comfortable.

"What can I do for you?" she said under her breath, a slight hint of annoyance in her voice.

"It's just a routine visit, Mrs. Cooper," Boris said affably. "We have a few questions to ask you and we'll be out your hair in no time."

He punctuated his sentence with a seductive smile that she didn't even seem to take into account.

"You got a warrant?"

A shadow passed over Pavlowski's face. Since she was obviously impervious to his charms, he didn't want to shatter the only tangible lead they had. "Mrs. Cooper," he repeated calmly, "we're on a high-profile criminal investigation, and our suspect's past has led us here. We were just hoping to get some information and, as I told you, we'll be out of here as soon as possible."

She crossed her arms and sank into her chair. Two signs that set off all the alarms in Michael's mind: she was putting herself in a position to refuse any co-operation. He noticed that every time Boris spoke her name, she slid her thumb over the inside of her left ring finger. A discreet and unconscious gesture. A fine trace of tan at the base of the finger confirmed to Michael that she must have recently worn a wedding ring. Was she in the middle of a divorce? Was the name Cooper that of a husband she was about to leave? It was time to save this interview from certain disaster.

"Madam," he said in a soft voice, "we have a certain Christopher Tremblay in custody in Rochester, and the Canadian police have sent us his file. It indicates that he spent three years in your unit."

She sighed and swiveled toward her computer. She moved both arms toward her keyboard and then stopped.

"I know my rights, gentlemen. I am bound by professional secrecy: I am not supposed to tell you anything."

Her non-verbal language betrayed her words. Her shoulders opened and her eyebrows arched and raised: her body showed her desire to help the two investigators, but her mind dictated that she should exert one last pressure, as a way of asserting herself as a director and not losing her authority by giving in quickly to the will of the two American cops.

Michael saw a gap where he could step in. "Our suspect has confessed to four murders, the case is serious. He won't say anything more and this hospital is the only tangible lead we have left."

He had voluntarily put himself in a position of submission, insisting that she was their last resort. It also played on the pride of the young woman who now saw herself as holding an important power: that of being the key element in a criminal investigation.

She stopped watching him and started typing on her keyboard. She entered Christopher Tremblay's name into the hospital database, and as she read the information on her screen, she looked stunned. "Your man was here, but that was almost five years ago! Unfortunately, I wasn't in charge of this unit at the time. It's difficult for me to give you any more information."

She seemed to be speaking only to Michael, and carefully avoided meeting Pavlowski's eyes. Boris quickly noticed that his alpha male ego was bruised. His colleague's smarmy tone was starting to annoy him. "Give us the name of the ones in charge at that time then," he said curtly.

She stiffened, looked for support in Michael's eyes in silence, then returned to her screen without a glance for Boris.

This mess has gone on too long.

"This is a police investigation, Mrs. Cooper; please do not obstruct it," Boris said, leaning his chest forward to bring his face closer to the young woman's.

"I agree to co-operate and to tell you all that I know, but I will not deliver the name of my colleagues like that, without their consent," she answered while shaking her head.

He tightened his fist and his jaw muscles contracted. "Mrs. Cooper, we have a suspect in custody who confessed several crimes, and we have nothing on him except the fact that he made a stay here following a court sentence. Please, help us."

Michael looked at the director's face and analyzed her actions: she was getting cold feet and was going to clam up like an oyster. Boris was screwing things up, but there was no way he was going to confront him in front of her. "Ma'am," he said in a soothing voice, "what my colleague is trying to tell you is that time is of the essence and if we leave here without more information, the suspect may be released and he's bound to reoffend."

She closed her eyes as if weighing the pros and cons in her mind, then shook her head again, her straight hair gently billowing like delicate silk curtains over her thin shoulders. "Come back with the Canadian police and I'll tell you everything you want to know," she concluded, crossing her arms.

Michael had understood that they would get nothing more out of her, the discussion was over. The two Americans were not on home turf and Mrs. Cooper was right: the cops should have been accompanied by representatives of the local authorities.

Michael stood up abruptly and signaled to Boris that it was time to leave. His colleague's fist remained clenched, and his knuckles were now white. "Very well then, there's no need to bother you any longer."

The face of the director lit up, she even repressed a smile. She was no doubt congratulating herself on the outcome of the interview; she had won this battle and was satisfied to have kept the authority that her position gave her. "I'll show you out, gentlemen," she said.

As she walked around her office, Pavlowski glared at her, his jaw still locked. Before passing the two men, she gave him one last look of superiority, which made him boil with rage.

During the whole walk to the lobby, he was sure that she had deliberately accentuated her height, in pure defiance. The automatic door opened and Mrs. Cooper stretched her arm out, directing the two visitors to step into the lobby. Her path ended there.

The receptionist looked up for a few seconds and then, with a jaded look, went back to her screen. The glass panel closed on the director and the two policemen faced their own reflections. Failure could be read on their faces.

Eager to leave the building, Boris accelerated his pace towards the exit. As for Michael, he was admiring the old stone vault which rose above them, and threaded slowly, scanning the various paintings which decorated the walls.

Oil-painted sailboats against a backdrop of raging seas, photographic prints under glass depicting other boats or marinas at sunset, and at the far end of the room, near the front door where Boris stood impatiently, the portrait of a man caught his eye.

He calmly walked over, looked at the picture, and then bent his head toward the text at the bottom of the frame. His eyes suddenly widened, and he made a hasty gesture with his hand to his teammate.

Intrigued, Boris approached him and looked down at the inscription Michael was pointing at. "There," he said.

In letters written in Indian ink, the two policemen could read the words that confirmed that they had not wasted their day by coming here.

The name underneath the portrait was unequivocal: Dr. Louis Becker, known as "the Captain."

17

___

"Still not done with your 'smoke break'," said Alsayed, miming quotation marks with his fingers.

Emma put down her puzzle book, dropped her pen, and gave her colleague a blasé look. "What do you want, Jamal?"

"Any news about this key thing?"

"Almeida is on it, going through all the comments under the post. You should see the number of ACABs, it's frightening."

He shrugged and his face took on an amused look. "*All Cops Are Bastards?* People don't like cops, that's a fact. I prefer hate speech to projectiles aimed at us when we're on the job though," he added.

"As far as I'm concerned, neither. I think it's a very serious matter that such slander can be committed with impunity."

"Freedom of speech," Jamal said with a sigh.

"If we let these people insult us without lifting a finger, we cultivate their hatred and, you know as well as I how far things can go."

Jamal squatted down to tie one of his shoelaces and then stood back up. "I know, Emma, don't forget that I'm a Muslim cop," he said.

"Don't forget that I am a woman," she retorted.

He seemed to take in the full scope of Emma's remarks, and nodded in agreement.

A few seconds passed before she broke the silence. "What's up on your side? The escort site, the pros?"

He shook his head. "Squat. The few girls we managed to reach out to know each other, but no one has ever heard of a Jenni Grosch-Steiner. Besides, without any pictures to show them, it didn't take us long to run out of arguments."

"Michael thinks that this guy, Bruno Costa, didn't tell us everything he knows. He'd like to interview him again."

"What? He wants us to call him back?" said Alsayed.

She nodded. "I don't think there's much to get out from him but I'm still convinced that there's something wrong with this Jenni."

"Female instinct?"

She opened her eyes wide and he burst out laughing. "I'm teasing you, sis!" he said, raising his arms in the air.

With a slight smile at the corner of her lips, she seized an eraser on the desk and threw it at her colleague. "Don't you have enough sisters as it is? Go back to work, lazy ass!"

Jamal walked away and Emma felt a chill run down her spine. Her female instinct, as Alsayed called it, often took this form. She was certain that Bruno Costa was hiding something from them and that there was an important detail hidden in the turpitude of his relationship with Jenni.

She approached Boris's office and borrowed the report on the search of the escort's house. She had been there, but wanted to see the scene again with fresh eyes. Crime Scene had frozen the place, so she immersed herself in the report to browse the apartment virtually. An elaborate technique that Michael had taught her.

It was a question of stabilizing her breathing, and focusing on her sensations, and to finally create a vacuum in her mind and project mental images of the place. For that, it was sometimes simpler to be helped by smells or sounds perceived during the first visit. She had already seen Michael take an object seized on site and smell it, most often under the stifled laughter of his fellow policemen.

Unfortunately, Emma had not imprinted any particular sound or smell in her mind at Jenni's house, but her memory of the room layout was still fresh. She closed her eyelids and concentrated. The extensive list of objects in the alleged victim's house helped her tremendously with the visualization exercise.

She saw herself in Jamal's company and revisited the place virtually. As with the search, she ended up in the bathroom, where the Bluestar had revealed pools of blood that someone had attempted to clean. She visualized the flowered shower curtain with a missing ring, the electric toothbrush on the edge of the sink, the toothpaste in an elephant-shaped container, the wicker laundry basket, the shampoos and body care products in the shower tray, the small white cabinet with drawers containing makeup, a hair straightener, a hair dryer, and cotton swabs. Mentally, she opened the drawer again and inspected the interior. Several lipsticks of different colors, lip gloss, the hair straightener, the hair dryer of the same brand and the box of cotton swabs. She felt that something was wrong, that she was about to find out what, and her eyelids twitched with concentration.

Suddenly she opened her eyes and smiled broadly.

Something about Jenni Grosch-Steiner was not right, and this seemingly small detail – found in her bathroom in particular – changed everything.

Her hands shaking with excitement, she grabbed her cell phone and dialed Michael's number.

On the highway to Rochester, Michael was speeding, about five miles per hour over the limit. The rain had stopped, but the sky still refused to let any sunlight through.

"Do you think this Becker has anything to do with our man?" asked Boris, still as puzzled as he had been since their visit to the psychiatric ward.

Without taking his eyes off the road, his partner answered him in a categorical tone. "When you interviewed Tremblay with Emma the first time, he did mention a 'captain,' didn't he?"

"Maybe it's a coincidence."

"So what? Let's find out what we can about this Louis Becker and see."

"In my opinion, it's a waste of time, I'd rather we focus on other leads," said Pavlowski.

"What leads?" asked his colleague, frowning.

"I've developed a theory. I didn't tell you about it earlier because I didn't have enough information, but it's becoming a little clearer now."

Michael's curiosity was piqued, but he remained silent.

"Aren't you hungry?" said Boris. "I've had nothing in my stomach since this morning: do you want to go and have a bite to eat and I'll tell you all about it then?"

The lieutenant's tone seemed strangely cordial to Michael, and he considered the offer for some time.

"I promised to have lunch with an old friend today. Sorry, but your theory will have to wait until I get back to the precinct."

"It's almost three o'clock," Pavlowski said with a grimace.

"You're right, I'm already very late."

The highway exit was approaching and Boris was lost in thought. The elusive Michael was giving him a hard time, and he wondered if he wasn't spending more time trying to understand this enigmatic human being than trying to solve the investigation they were working on. All in all, he remained convinced that Michael was linked to the case, and he was impatient to get to the bottom of it and expose him.

As the buildings of the Rochester barracks came into view behind the plane trees of the avenue leading to them, Michael came out of another silence. "Can I drop you off at the gate? I really have to go. I'll see you in an hour."

Under other circumstances, Pavlowski would never have let a policeman under his command lead his own life in the middle of a criminal investigation, but in this case, he needed to back off in order to gain his trust. Let him go to lunch in the middle of the afternoon if he wanted to, Michael couldn't avoid the next step.

18

After Boris got out of the car, Michael turned the car around and, when he was out of sight of his colleague, he reached for his bottle of anti-anxiety drugs and swallowed a pill that scraped his windpipe. He felt it slide all the way down to his stomach.

At a red light, he tipped his head back on the headrest and closed his eyes. Shadows danced under his eyelids, and he could feel his heartbeat slowing.

A few seconds later, horns startled him out of his thoughts. He drove off, his tires squealing on the asphalt, still soaking wet from the rain.

About five miles further, the road curved and would keep winding for the last few minutes of the trip. The surrounding green nature was dueling against the darkness of the sky. There were no houses around, just trees as far as the eye could see. Only the buds that adorned oaks, chestnut trees and larches gave the landscape a semblance of hope in this gloomy setting.

Around a bend in the road, rain-soaked ruts – probably left by a tractor – confirmed the presence of humans in this part of the backcountry.

He slowed the car down at the beginning of a gravel road that sloped gently down to a rustic lodge, whose two roof edges touched the ground. The wood of the façade and the balcony looked outdated, and only the tiles had retained the brilliance of the early days.

When he opened the car door, the cold rushed inside, reminding him with icy caresses that far from the city, the temperature had dropped a few more degrees. The scent of the gentians, which decorated a corner of the garden left to abandon, evoked happy memories of adolescence. Reflexively, he glanced at the rusty portico that had once held a trapeze and a swing, and a slight twinge of pain gripped his heart. Under normal circumstances, his hypersensitivity would have caused an unpleasant lump in his throat and an irrepressible urge to cry, but thanks to the chemical assistance of the anxiolytics, the discomfort was diffused and seemed far away.

Posted in front of the entrance, he pressed the doorbell and waited a few seconds. The little red curtain behind the window in the center of the wooden panel parted and he caught a glimpse of Henry Saget's smile.

"It's about time!" exclaimed the former captain as he opened the door.

He held out his arms, inviting Michael into a warm embrace. Michael rushed to greet his host.

Inside, the furniture was kept to a minimum, leaving as much room as possible for the book-laden shelves that covered almost the entire surface of the wall. Several low-voltage bulbs diffused a warm and welcoming orange light. The old wooden floor creaked under the two men's footsteps as they made their way to a large room, in the center of which a chessboard seemed to be patiently waiting for someone to pay attention to it.

Michael leaned over the board and inspected the configuration of the pieces. "You still haven't played?"

Henry answered from the adjoining kitchen, from where he brought in a steaming pot of tea and two cups. "I was waiting for you! I'd rather you see my next move with your very eyes. You won't sleep at night ever again."

He laughed loudly, while Michael just smiled shyly.

"Would you like some tea?" Henry asked.

"Same brand as last time?"

"The same!" he declared proudly. "Icy Embrace."

"Icy Embrace it is then. Even if it's risky given these temperatures!"

"Do you want to see my master move?" asked Henry, pointing to the chess set.

"Later, maybe," Michael replied, scratching the top of his head, immediately regretting the gesture, which an expert like him would have interpreted as embarrassment.

Saget frowned. "Is everything okay? Did your return to the precinct go well?"

Nothing could be hidden from the former Rochester PD boss, and although he had not received the same courses as the synergologist, he was still a keen observer, as well as a perceptive man with sharp senses.

Michael blew on his cup before answering. "I'm all right. It's just that we're on a strange case..."

Henry left his chair and returned to the kitchen. "Come to think of it," he said, "I saved you some leftovers from lunch. I had to eat without you, I hope you don't mind. Rice with portobello mushrooms and soy steak. No butter, no cream."

The anti-anxiety medication made Michael feel like his head was wrapped with layers of cotton, and the hunger that had been tugging at his stomach a few hours before had completely disappeared. "I'll take it all back to the station later," he replied.

Again, the former captain's face darkened. He came back to the room slowly; the floor creaked. He sank into the worn velvet of an armchair and looked at Michael. "A strange case, you say?" he asked.

Michael took another sip and focused on the warm feeling that slid down his throat. "A strange guy shows up yesterday in a small precinct around Rochester and says he's killed four people. He won't say his name, or why he did it, and starts writing down a list of his four victims."

Henry's eyes widened and he settled more comfortably into his seat.

"There was no way to get him to say anything during the interviews, so we looked for the names on the list and found out where the victims lived. Again, very strange... Traces of blood that were cleaned, but no bodies."

"Profiles of the victims?"

"A trader, an escort girl, a YouTuber and a composer."

"Unusual," says Henry, scratching his clean-shaven cheek. "Is there anything connecting them?"

Michael sighed and looked up. His gaze wandered to the hundreds of books that lined the large bookcase at the back of the room. Mostly mystery novels, but also old books, classics of literature. He wandered for a few seconds, his mind clouded by the painkillers, and then came to. "Lotus flower carpet, meditation bell..."

At the mention of these words, Henry Saget stiffened, but seeing that Michael did not seem to have finished, he let him continue.

"That's not all," he said after swallowing with difficulty, "in the few personal effects of the suspect, we found a business card with the logo of The Children of Gaïa."

The retired captain jumped out of his seat and clenched his jaws. Michael heard him grunt as he paced back and forth, pounding the air with his clenched fist. Henry walked over to one of the windows, overlooking the entire valley, and scanned the horizon.

"Fuck... here we go again..." he mumbled over and over again, his forehead against the glass. He quickly pulled himself together and pivoted towards Michael. "Do you think *they* sent him? How did this guy end up at the Rochester PD?"

"He turned himself in at the Bloomfield PD, and they made the custody transfer right away," Michael replied.

Henry took a few steps toward his nephew, his eyebrows furrowed and his face serious. "Show me his face!"

Michael grabbed his cell phone and searched its electronic memory. He retrieved the file and displayed the suspect's picture on the screen. "His name is Christopher Tremblay, and he's Canadian."

Saget squinted his eyes and moved his head closer to the smartphone. "A junkie?" he asked.

"He's been attending sessions of The Children of Gaïa program for addicts. He's probably unbalanced. He spent three years in a psychiatric ward after stabbing people in the street."

"How long ago was that?" Henry asked, still tense.

"Five years ago."

The retired captain suddenly seemed calmed by the information, his features relaxed, and he agreed to sit back down. He grabbed his cup of tea and soothed his dry throat. "Tell me about the victims, will you?"

"We don't know much. They're almost ghosts. Nothing from social security, nothing from the IRS: just electricity bills and unidentified bank accounts."

"Telephone bills?" asked Henry, reverting to his old investigator's reflexes.

"No cell phones were found in the various homes. The four apartments belong to the same real estate company."

Astonished, his interlocutor opened his eyes wide and

dropped his jaw. "That's strange..." He scratched the top of his head through his silver hair before continuing. "Names?"

Even though he knew them by heart, Michael glanced at the notes on his smartphone. "Colin Vassard is the trader; Jenni Grosch-Steiner is the escort; then we have Tod Sheepmann who is presumably a composer and Slevin Bradich who makes his living making videos about a popular online game."

Henry's bushy eyebrows, as silver as his hair, twisted into a worried frown. As he remained silent, Michael continued, "Does it remind you of something?" he asked.

Henry shook his head as if coming out of a bad dream. "No, nothing. The names, I mean..."

Michael knew him well, and knew that when he stared off into the distance, leaving long pauses between his words, it was because he had an idea brewing in his mind. The detective had learned a great deal from him, and in the most complex investigations, he learned most about his mentor and his way of thinking and working. The look on his face betrayed a concern that never boded well.

"But?" Michael insisted.

"But the method reminds me of something. You tell me that the names lead to a dead end?"

"To not much anyway. I told you, nothing from IRS nor the social services: that's what we usually encounter with illegal immigrants, but our four victims have nothing to do with these kinds of people."

"You don't know anything about it. After all, you have no clues, do you? Any pictures?"

Michael shook his head.

Henry leaned back in his chair and continued to rub his face.

"I know you, when you're like this, you're thinking about something," said Michael.

"Of course I'm thinking about something, everyone is thinking about something!" said the ex-cop, punctuating his sentence with a wink. He sighed and his shoulders heaved. "You haven't come across any classified material yet?"

"What do you mean? Secret Service? Army?" Michael asked, suddenly intrigued.

"Maybe. Your victims look like ghosts to me, and ghosts, except in children's stories, are found in witness protection cases."

A door suddenly opened in the detective's mind, giving free access to new leads. Too obsessed by the link that the investigation had with the cult in which he had spent his early youth, he had almost obscured certain possibilities that had been touched upon before.

"What makes you say that?" Michael asked.

"I don't know, a hunch," Henry answered, tapping his nose with his index finger. "The names are weird, don't you think? Besides, it's strange that you can't find anything about the victims."

"That would explain why the same real estate company owns their homes..."

"I'll bet they're being fed, housed and laundered at taxpayers' expense."

Appearing concerned, Michael wore a grimace that made him look darker, almost angry. He shook his head slowly from side to side. "I don't have as much experience as you do," he said, "but it still seems far-fetched. What kind of prosecution would justify such a deployment of resources?"

"Who's talking about a prosecution? It could very well be the result of an ongoing investigation," the former captain retorted.

"What? Involving politics? Drug trafficking? Where would the orders come from? And above all, who has the means?"

"CIA, FBI, Army, you name it. I have old friends there; if you want, I can give them a call. They won't say anything, but I can tell them about your case, and they could at least tell me if that kind of thing is possible or not."

"I'll email you the file then."

Michael's smartphone suddenly vibrated. Emma's name appeared on the screen. He turned it on silent mode and put the phone back in his pocket.

"Aren't you going to take the call?" Henry asked, surprised.

"I'm already several hours late for our lunch, so I'm not going to spend my time on the phone when we haven't seen each other for two months."

"So I'll save my killer move for another time," said Henry with a smile.

"I feel like this game will never end."

"If you play every two months, that's for sure!" Henry said, giving a friendly tap on the shoulder of his nephew.

The implicit evocation of his absence of over sixty days seemed to suddenly affect Henry. He paused for a moment and, not wanting to let silence weigh down what he thought was a too-rare, convivial moment, he filled Michael's cup once again.

The detective watched the wisps of smoke rise above the greenish liquid. "Thank you for everything you've done," said Michael in a soft voice. "I know I've been out of the loop all this time and haven't really had a chance to tell you, but thanks."

"You're welcome, Mike."

"I'm sorry I put you in an uncomfortable position." He took a hot sip and continued. "I really lost it, Henry. This whole thing has made me crazy," he admitted sheepishly.

"I know, I know. Don't worry, I understood why you had a fit and I made sure your record stayed clean of it. Times have changed: in my day, something like this would never have happened."

Michael whispered another "thank you" and turned to Saget, flashing an attempted smile.

The former captain stood up and headed to the kitchen, teapot and cups in hand. Michael pulled his smartphone from his pocket and glanced at the notifications: six missed calls, all from Emma. A slight shiver of worry tickled the back of his neck; he sensed that something important was going on at the station.

Henry reappeared in the doorway and his guest looked at him. "Emma keeps trying to reach me," Michael told his uncle.

"Call her back, don't mind me."

He had blinked several times, and Michael immediately knew that the slight hint of disappointment he had detected in his voice was real.

As he left the room, trying to contain his impatience, he dialed his colleague's number. Barely one ring later and she picked up. "It's about time, what the hell are you doing?" Emma asked.

"What's going on?"

"I think I know who Jenni Grosch-Steiner is!"

19

———

In Assia's office, the air smelled like burnt plastic. The odor was due to the small heater she was using while waiting for the building's heating to be turned back on. Warm memories of Hawaii suddenly resurfaced. She saw herself and two of her brothers coming home from school on the last day of class before the Christmas holidays in the warmth of Honolulu. She smiled at the idea that a few years later, to the day, she experienced snow for the first time in her life, when a beautiful white sheet covered the roofs and streets of Rochester and its suburbs. Traffic had slowed to a crawl and the bitter cold forced passersby to wrinkle their noses and burrow their faces into their coats. Assia had stood there, in the middle of the roadway amidst the sounds of horns and traffic, her head tilted back and her tongue sticking out, letting the snowflakes melt gently on her face. It was one of her most beautiful memories after leaving her home state.

She was angry at herself for having gotten used to all this and for having finally adopted the plaintive attitude that she attributed – not without mockery – to the *mainlanders*.

She glanced at the blasting heater and thought to herself

that, in her defense, the temperatures in this early spring were totally abnormal. The morning's weather report even predicted snow at medium altitudes in the coming days.

Assia lost herself in her thoughts, between images of bad weather and reminiscences of her childhood, then this stream of thoughts was interrupted by a vision of Michael's face. Mixed feelings seized her. She imagined him teaming up with Boris for the needs of the investigation, and remembered instantaneously the request that the tall blond had made to her. She hadn't had time to look more closely at this matter of protected files and had given Lieutenant Pavlowski full access to all of them.

Piqued by curiosity, she shook her mouse to turn back on her idle computer and began a search of all the files that had been granted Level 2 security.

The hard drive emitted brief electronic crackles and the result of her query stimulated her interest furthermore. Only one file was protected by this restriction and she clicked on it.

It was the minutes of a report of the search of The Children of Gaïa's domain and the various statements made during the interviews. It would have taken too much time to read everything, so she skimmed the dozens of pages, promising herself to print it out and read it in detail when she had the chance. The facts, though nearly thirty years old, were intertwined with Michael's story, and that's precisely what worried her.

She then took the liberty of studying the report drawn up following Michael's burnout. According to his superior at the time, Captain Henry Saget, he had become too emotionally involved in a case of alleged rape of a young girl, just over eighteen years of age, who had not dared to file a complaint until very late in the day. Officially, the fact that the suspect had been released very quickly for lack of substantial evidence had caused Detective Monroe to lose his temper, and he had thrown an unprecedented fit. Some officers of the station had to intervene and to try to reason with him. Captain Saget suggested that Michael take some time off to rest, and the detective agreed. From higher up in the hierarchy, it was required that he undergo a psychological follow-up, which he also accepted.

The whole process seemed too easy to be true to Assia. She couldn't claim to know Michael in depth, but something told her that the portrait of him that was painted in this file made him seem far too docile. Michael Monroe was not one to be tamed that easily. Even if Henry Saget, who had played the role of Michael's mentor, had been there to calm him down, she had difficulty imagining that the lines she read on the report transcribed the whole truth. There had to be another side to the story, and she intended to go all the way to find out.

She grabbed her cell phone and typed a message to Michael.

Tonight? Your place?

Despite the question marks, it was not a request, more an order.

His jacket zipped all the way up, Boris walked across the Rochester PD parking lot towards the station. His imposing build, height and proud gait gave him the look of an ideal military man, or at least the image that civilians had of them.

Barely noticing his colleagues and without removing his coat, he headed for his desk, unlocked one of the drawers with a small key, and grabbed a packet of printed papers.

Under the discreet gazes of his fellow policemen who wondered what he was up to, he made his way through the building's maze of corridors and isolated himself in an interview room. His empty stomach called out for help, and he regretted not stopping at the pizzeria across the street for a snack. The pizzas weren't great, but the establishment had the merit of serving food from 11:00am to midnight non-stop. However, if the feeling of hunger became too strong, he would ask one the Blues to get him something to eat.

He sat down on a chair that creaked under his weight. He slammed the stack of papers down in front of him and concentrated.

In a silence occasionally broken by the flickering of a neon light that would likely soon stop working, he read and reread, sometimes three or four times, the different parts of the file classified Level 2 to which his superior had granted him access. He now had clear proof: the name of Michael Monroe did not appear anywhere, and that was more than strange.

His colleague had confessed to him to have lived within the cult of The Children of Gaïa and, at the time of a big operation which aimed at searching the whole domain, the members of the Monroe family were listed. Mary, his mother, Frank, his father and Ellie, an eighteen-year-old girl. But no trace of Michael. How was it possible? The report dated from 1998, he must have been barely fifteen years old at the time: how could he not be present if everyone else was there? There was always the possibility that he had been taken out of the hands of the cult and placed in a foster home before the facts, but Boris had trouble placing the hypothesis in his mind.

He sighed and looked up at the ceiling as if he would find an answer there. He thought for several minutes and then suddenly had an idea.

Determined, he took his smartphone out of his inside jacket pocket and launched the internet browser. He ran a search on The Children of Gaïa cult and narrowed the results to the Rochester area and the 1990s.

A satisfied grin appeared at the corner of his mouth when he came across a website whose name, cult-warning.org, was unmistakable. It listed an impressive number of cults and sectarian movements that had existed in the US or were still active there.

In a column on the right-hand side of the page, various designations were listed in alphabetical order. He clicked on "Children of Gaia (the)" and a small gleam came to his eyes at the sight of the amount of information that was displayed before him.

The work had been colossal and meticulous: newspaper clippings over almost thirty years, testimonies of repentant cult members and, in some cases, even photocopied and digitized investigation reports.

Browsing through the articles like a bee foraging from flower to flower, his gaze was quickly drawn to a case dating from the early 2000s, in which the cult was implicated.

In essence, the cult was accused of using a complex method of attracting new followers by making their old lives "disappear". It provided these people with a new identity, a new temporary home and, gradually, all traces of their past were carefully erased. Those who had a job negotiated a severance – with the help of lawyers paid directly by the cult – and transferred their unemployment benefits to an untraceable account held by a screen company belonging to The Children of Gaïa. All savings and possible stock portfolios were transferred there as well.

Pavlowski made the connection with their ongoing investigation. The four victims on Christopher Tremblay's list seemed to be living on the fringes of society in housing that was all owned by the same real estate company, and the money that some of them earned – like Vassard or Bradich – was paid into obscure accounts. This practice had all the appearance of a similar MO. He had to immediately notify Alsayed and

Almeida's teams to let them know about this discovery. However, his train of thought stopped short at Michael Monroe. Boris was convinced that he was involved in this case, or at least that it had something to do with his mysterious past in the cult. He would have greatly preferred that his colleagues follow this new lead in secret, but Emma wouldn't be able to refrain from telling her friend about it.

If he decided to act alone, Pavlowski would have little room for maneuver, especially since he wanted Detective Monroe close to him in order to watch his every move. As soon as Michael got back to the precinct, Boris would not let him out of sight.

Pavlowski saved the website to his favorites, gathered up the papers scattered on the room's only table, and decided to keep all this information to himself. He would follow up on The Children of Gaïa's lead with Michael, and when he'd learned enough, he would go to Assia Jenkins and tell her what he had found.

This low blow would surely earn him the animosity of the whole precinct, but the case was too serious: four victims were possibly between life and death at this time, and a cop might have been involved. The investigation could not move forward under such pernicious conditions. It was necessary to get rid of the pest before rebuilding on a sound foundation.

The ringing of his phone startled him, and when he saw the caller ID, he thought the devil himself was reading his mind. It was Michael.

"Yes?" he said, picking up.

"Where are you? I'm back at the station, Emma found something."

20

"It's about time!" Emma shouted as Michael entered the open space, her mouth full of a piece of sandwich.

He looked around the huge room and looked surprised. "Where's Boris?" he asked.

"Are you missing him already?" said the beautiful redhead, triggering a few laughs.

"I'm here!"

Sergeant Pavlowski had just appeared. The tone of his voice cut through Emma's banter, and the hubbub died down, as if a king had burst into the room and overheard rumors of a plot against him.

Michael waited for his colleague to join him, and the two of them moved toward Emma's office. She was now sharing her snack with Jamal. Michael thought to himself that the cops never ate at decent hours. He himself still hadn't eaten anything since the morning, and his lunch patiently awaited him on the passenger seat of his car, in a Tupperware box.

With a closed, authoritative expression on his face, Boris didn't give him a chance to carry on a conversation, and he struck the first blow. "You've got news, King, right?"

Everyone noticed the use of the surname, but Emma did not blink and instead showed a big smile before answering. "Exactly!" she said.

She got up quickly, swept the crumbs off the tray on her desk, wrapped the rest of her sandwich in the aluminum foil that had been used to carry it, and held up a thin file consisting of a few printed sheets.

"Look," she went on, "I've read and reread the search report dozens of times, and there's something weird. Already, when Jamal and I went to Jenni Grosch-Steiner's house, I had a bad feeling, a feeling that something was missing."

She held the file out to the two men and pointed to an area of text. "Here is the description of the place and the list of all the objects that were in the apartment. I'm not going to play guessing games, but I can assure you that no woman lives there."

Curiosity changed the expression on Boris's and Michael's faces. As usual, Michael was not very demonstrative, but the change in his features was noticeable enough to confirm to Emma that he was curious.

"What makes you say that?" asked Boris, impatient.

"The whole apartment, and the whole bathroom, is missing something a woman needs once a month."

Michael frowned.

"Feminine hygiene products?"

"Yep, tampons, pads, cups, you name it," she replied. "All women have it at home, at their partners' houses, in their purses, even at their parents' houses! There's not even a Midol or an Advil, nothing. Either this Jenni hasn't gone through puberty, or there's something else going on, but I find it strange."

The males around considered what Emma had just said. There was silence between them for a few seconds, then Boris spoke. "It's been established that this woman is a prostitute; maybe she's only using her downtown apartment for her sexual encounters. She's just 'working' there, if you will. And I doubt she goes there during her bad week."

Her bad week? *What a douche*, Emma thought. But Pavlowski's intervention had made her wonder: maybe he wasn't totally wrong.

Michael grabbed the file and looked at its contents. He absentmindedly walked off toward his desk like a zombie before the stunned eyes of his two colleagues.

He sat down in his chair, put the few sheets in front of him and reached for his Rubik's cube. His fingers mechanically manipulated the faces of the puzzle, the colored squares flashing up before his eyes. He was so used to solving the different combinations that his hands were on autopilot, and his mind could escape the tumult of extraneous thoughts and focus on the essential.

What if Emma was onto something? Why wouldn't a woman have something in her home to protect her clothing during her period? There was an infinite number of possibilities, an infinite number of coincidences: not everything followed an immutable logic, and sometimes the simplest explanations were the closest to the truth. Perhaps Jenni Grosch-Steiner had run out of menstrual protection items that day. Could the answer be that clear?

The first white side of the cube was done, and he was about to tackle the first crown when he suddenly hit the desk with the palm of his hand. He dropped his toy and launched the internet browser on his computer. Boris gave Emma an inquiring look; she responded with a shrug, letting him know that she was used to Michael's strange behavior after all these years.

"Are you going to tell us what you're doing?" Pavlowski grumbled, on the verge of annoyance.

"I might have an idea," he said softly. "Come over here."

The tall blond man moved with long strides, followed by Emma, the gleam in her eyes betraying her excitement.

Michael did not wait for his two colleagues to join him, and entered the address of the escort website. He moved his mouse icon over a location filter named "Rochester" and clicked. The number of entries was drastically reduced; he checked the list of all the profiles again. Still the same, still no Jenni.

Scanning the screen, his gaze stopped on the three tabs at the top of the page. By default, searches were done under the one tab that read "Girls". The next one was reserved for clients who preferred affairs with men, but it was the last one that interested Michael. He moved his mouse over the text, which changed color to a bluish tint.

He had just clicked on "Shemales & CD".

In this particular field, the offer was reduced to only three profiles. He scrolled through them, and one of them caught his attention. It had an unmistakable name: Jenn GS.

The photo showed a woman in a nun's fetish outfit with her face blurred out.

"I don't get it," said Pavlowski, looking confused.

"Emma was right," Michael replied, "Jenni Grosch-Steiner is actually a man."

Boris was having a hard time wrapping his head around the idea, and the pictures on the website weren't helping him sort things out. Jenni had all the hallmarks of a beautiful woman; tall and slim, almost a model's look; long slender legs with a curve accentuated by high heels, and a sleek body in a tight costume which stuck to her skin. Of course, a circle blurred her face, but just from the sight of her sensual morphology and her very feminine way of posing, Boris remained disconcerted.

"I could feel that Costa was hiding something from us," Michael continued. "His posture and gestures expressed shame, and when he finally admitted that he was seeing an escort girl, I chalked it up to embarrassment. But there was more to him than that…"

Emma leaned over the desk and grabbed the mouse. She scrolled through all the profile pictures, five in all, then stood up. "You guys not only get paid more," she said, "but you make some damn fine chicks! It's really not fair."

Embarrassed by the contradictory feelings that were flooding his mind, Boris did not pick up on the joke and remained frozen at the screen. As for Michael, he'd long since lost the desire to joke about it.

"Do you think she… he's dressed up like a woman or…?"

"Does she still have one or not?" Emma said. "You can say it, you know."

Boris ran a hand through his golden hair.

"Basically," Emma continued, "if he… she takes a hormonal treatment and has the will to go through a sex change, she's transgender; but if it's just a guy who likes to put on girl's clothes and a wig for his own pleasure, then it's what you call a cross-dresser."

After her explanation, Boris's face became darker. "Thank you, Detective King, I know the difference. Anyway, what does it change for us?"

"Not much indeed," admitted Michael, suddenly coming out of his silence. "But we do have one more clue: a phone number."

He scrolled through the various pages of Jenni's profile again and returned to the first one.

"Wait!" Emma thundered, moving forward. "Go back to the second-to-last photo."

Perplexed, he complied and her friend brought her face closer to the screen. "Can you zoom in?" she asked.

He double-clicked and suddenly understood what she had spotted.

The cold blade of anguish cut into his gut and his pulse raced.

"There," said Emma, pointing to a corner of the picture. "Do you see it?"

Michael could see it very well, unfortunately. He had paid little attention to details and, even if his intuition had suggested something familiar in the setting chosen by Jenni for her photo shoot, his conscience had covered it up like a body bag over a corpse that he did not want to see. However, nothing had escaped the sharp eye of Detective King.

"On the back wall," said Emma, "we can see the name of the place where these pictures were taken. It's Gravity Zero!"

Gravity Zero. At the mention of the name, a shiver of uneasiness ran through Michael's body, starting from the back of his neck and spreading to the ends of his limbs.

"What is this place?" asked Boris.

"A club. A swingers' club, and also an S&M club, you get the drift. We did a raid there a few years ago," Emma replied. "Nothing too crazy though. The boss never forgets to renew his license, and we found dope on some clients, like in any nightclub in the country."

"This is a strong lead anyway," said Pavlowski. "You and Alsayed, go there and ask around. Even if we can't see her face clearly, print out the pictures and ask who might recognize her. I'd like to know when this shoot took place too."

Michael, until then silent and frozen like a statue, shivered when Boris put a hand on his shoulder. "As for us, let's go pay a visit to Costa," he resumed, "and we're going to worm everything out of him that we need to know. He lied to us, and I want to make sure he's not hiding anything else."

As Michael left the open space, he crossed paths with Assia. The tender look she gave him, as brief as it was, comforted him a little. He waved to her so discreetly that he wasn't even sure she saw it.

Outside, the gloomy weather weighed on his mind like a growing burden. Boris was already far away, diving into his vehicle, but Michael, short of breath, had to stop halfway. The scenery around him began to flicker, and he felt nauseous. He leaned forward, bent his knees and put his hands on his thighs as if he were about to bow to some god in the middle of the parking lot.

Maybe Assia was right after all, he wasn't back on track yet. He had the unpleasant feeling that this case had caught him in the mouth of a gigantic monster and that it was digesting him, crushing him little by little. First The Children of Gaïa, then his parents, and now the only place where he felt free to be himself: Gravity Zero.

A thick, dark mist hovered over him like a circle of hungry vultures, hoping for the slightest sign of weakness to swoop down on him and suffocate him.

An icy gust slapped him in the face and, somehow, he pulled himself together. He felt the sudden need to swing by his car and get his medication. Could he ever do without it?

He came back to an impatient Boris, who sped off as soon as he closed the door. The GPS in the dashboard showed the address of Bruno Costa's workplace, a downtown supermarket.

Pavlowski remained silent the whole way, which suited Michael perfectly as he waited for the chemical molecules of the anti-anxiety drugs to diffuse throughout his body. He checked the driving time and sighed with relief. When they arrived at their destination, the pressure on his chest would be completely gone. He knew he wouldn't be in full possession of his senses for the interview with Costa, but that would be more than enough to decipher the gestural tics of a guy who wasn't – unlike the thugs who regularly fell into the cops' net – used to interviews.

The supermarket was located in an ultra-modern shopping mall that looked like it had sprouted like a wart in the middle of Rochester's historic center. The metal-and-glass structure housed about a hundred shops that lined up on either side of a central aisle. For convenience, a huge parking lot had been dug in the bowels of the city to accommodate the ever-increasing influx of shoppers from the surrounding areas.

The two men walked among the crowd of shoppers, and Michael wondered for a second if the people around them saw them as cops. He looked at his partner and got his answer. Towering at six-foot-six, Boris certainly didn't go unnoticed, and his military-looking haircut couldn't fool anyone for long.

The two officers entered the supermarket and looked around. Bruno Costa had indicated that he was a cashier, and they looked to see if he was at his register.

In the distance, at checkout number 8, a thin, stunted figure was scanning an old woman's purchases in front of him, from right to left.

Boris indicated the direction to Michael with a short move of the chin. He walked down the aisles toward their target and grabbed a bottle of mineral water as he went, Michael following.

Like two disciplined customers, they lined up at checkout number 8, and when the little old lady finished paying for her groceries, the conveyor belt started moving, sending the plastic bottle towards Costa, who hadn't looked up.

"Hi," he said mechanically in a weak voice.

"Hello, Bruno," replied Pavlowski.

At the mention of his name, the cashier raised his head and

Michael watched his pupils dilate in the moment. A burst of adrenaline had awakened all his senses.

"Can you take a break?" Boris asked as Costa passed the item through the barcode scanner.

"Uh... what do you mean?" he said, baffled.

"We need to talk to you," Michael interjected. "We thought it would be better to do this on your break than to handcuff you in front of everyone and book you in."

Bruno Costa seemed about to fall apart, and his already greasy forehead was now glistening with sweat. He looked down and pressed a button. The light at the cashier's entrance turned from green to red and he stood up. He pulled himself out from behind the conveyor belt and away from the two officers before turning around.

"Follow me," he whispered.

Respecting his obvious desire for discretion and noting that he was co-operative, they followed him while remaining at a good distance.

When they reached a door whose color blended with the walls of the store, Costa passed his badge over a magnetic reader and unlocked it. Looking more and more worried, he invited the investigators to accompany him.

"I only get fifteen minutes every two hours," he said sheepishly, before entering an area that was presumably used as an employee break room.

"That's more than enough... if you co-operate," Boris said, inviting him to take a seat.

"I... I don't understand. What do you want from me?"

"The truth," Michael replied.

He noticed that the man sat with his feet in a firm position, his toes pointed on the floor, as opposed to the rest of his body which was in a more relaxed state. This immediately indicated to the synergologist that he was trying to pretend he was relaxed, while internal body tension was pulling at him.

"We're missing some details, Bruno," Michael said. "You have to tell us everything you know about Jenni."

As soon as he finished his sentence, he observed Costa's brief flickering gaze, a bit like a boomerang, which certainly demonstrated that he was withholding information. Cognitively, the interviewee had visualized something he wanted to hide. The two officers knew what it was, but they wanted to hear it from him. Michael, for his part, was hoping to decipher the cashier's systemic reactions to make sure he wasn't hiding anything else important from them.

Bruno remained silent, almost absent though his facial muscles succumbed to a series of nervous tics.

"We looked everywhere for Jenni, we went to the website you indicated to us, but we found nothing. Do you have an explanation?"

"I don't know, maybe she deleted her profile," he said, spreading his hands.

Michael was now certain that Bruno Costa was in a state of active focus: his upper body and his face were trying to fool them, while underneath the surface, the tension was palpable. He was ashamed of what he would have to reveal to the police, he was ashamed of himself. His secret had been discovered and he had reverted to childish reflexes, as if being questioned by his parents.

"Bruno," Michael calmly resumed, "your behavior betrays you. I can read you like an open book. You know that everything you say to us is completely confidential, right? Nobody has the right to break the laws that protect your privacy, you know?"

The cashier nodded and Michael noticed that he had put his feet flat on the floor. He was letting off steam.

"We are looking for Jenni Grosch-Steiner everywhere. It's a

criminal investigation and, if we want to find her, we can't afford half the truth, don't you agree? The facts are serious, we're doing everything we can to solve this case. To be honest, we don't care what you do in the privacy of your home. As long as you don't do anything illegal, it's not our problem. We just want you to tell us everything about her, okay? Everything."

Costa sighed and wiped the sweat from his face with the sleeve of his uniform shirt. His expression had changed completely, and Boris was forced to acknowledge his colleague's psychological work. They were now facing a completely different person.

"Jenni is, um, not really a woman," Bruno said.

Michael slowly closed his eyelids in a feline fashion, and Costa realized he could continue.

"I don't know if that's what you wanted to know... I didn't think it was really important. But we didn't... well, I never..."

"Who cares?" said Pavlowski, cutting him off. "Your sexual fantasies are not the object of our investigation."

The harsh tone had briefly made the man tense up and Michael gritted his teeth. His teammate was not really compatible with his methods, and he missed his tandem with Emma. Behind her rough-and-tumble demeanor, she was an ideal partner in this kind of situation. Boris, on the other hand, trampled on his work with his big hooves and didn't make it easier for him.

"This Jenni," continued Boris, "do you know her real name?"

"Uh... I've always called her that."

"What we want, Mr. Costa, is to find out her real civil status."

The little man frowned.

"According to you, was she transitioning?"

"I don't get it," he said, his face tense.

Michael wanted to intervene, but he risked destabilizing their interlocutor even more. The intimidating tone Boris was using was certainly not right for the situation, especially with a fragile person like Bruno Costa; but Michael had succeeded in making him open up to them, so his colleague would just have to finish the job his way, and it would still work.

"Was Jenni pre- or post-op? Was she taking any medication?" Lieutenant Pavlowski asked.

"Uh, no," Costa replied, looking down and clasping his hands together under the table. "She wasn't a... she was, let's say, more of an androgynous, effeminate person who liked to dress as a woman and..."

"And you never knew her name? Her man's name, I mean."

He shook his head.

He wasn't lying.

Michael was sure now; they would get nothing more out of Bruno Costa.

21

B ack at the precinct, Boris had called all the investigation teams into the room they had been using from the very beginning of the case.

The whiteboard entries were still asking the same questions, and as Michael entered the room, he was overwhelmed with a sense of failure that no answers had really been forthcoming at this point.

Boris seemed more nervous than usual, more authoritative as well, and from the questioning looks of his colleagues, Michael realized that they had never seen him like this either.

Boris didn't wait for everyone to take a seat around the big table before speaking. "Our four victims are finally four persons of the same gender! Four men! Detective Monroe and I confirmed this a few minutes ago. I've come up with some theories, and I'd like to discuss them in order to move this mysterious case into high gear."

The sound of chairs being scraped across the floor drowned out the sound of his voice, so he paused for a moment before continuing. "First, the profile of our suspect. Christopher

Tremblay has already spent time in a psychiatric unit in Canada following a violent stabbing incident. I have every reason to believe that he has done it again here with the four people he jotted down on that list. The shadow of The Children of Gaïa cult hangs over this whole case, and I would like us to dig deep into their recruitment methods and look for any laws they might be breaking in their operations."

At the mention of the name, Michael thought the audience would turn on him. Fortunately, no one flinched. The anti-anxiety medication kept him in a hazy state all afternoon, but it obviously didn't calm down his paranoia.

"A few years ago," Boris continued, "this cult had already been convicted of breach of trust and tax fraud following the discovery of an MO that I'm sure will remind you all of something. They make their followers change their identity, go away for a few months and then disappear from the face of the earth to go and hide in one of the many estates belonging to the cult. The leaders had thought of everything and made sure to convince their members to deposit all their money in almost untraceable offshore accounts. King, you told us about accounts with unknown IBANs, right?"

"That's right," she replied quickly. "Fischer and Almeida are on it." She made a brief movement of her chin in the direction of the two imposing officers.

Pablo was the first to speak. "We just got more details about this," he said, slightly puffing out his chest. He then opened a small moleskin notebook and turned a few pages. "The IBAN of the account to which the trader, Colin... er, Vassard, was transferring his money is Swiss, and the reason it didn't match anything we already had in our databases is that it came from an internet-only bank called Revolut."

Intrigued by this revelation, the audience now seemed captivated.

"In fact," Almeida continued, "Revolut is a British bank, but it provides its customers with several IBANs. They have partnerships in a lot of countries, and they offer account numbers that allow you to receive money in all the corresponding currencies, which is pretty convenient. And it's all free!" he said with a smile.

He let the silence settle for a few moments, then resumed. "And this is where it gets interesting. The other IBAN that we had identified, and which was used by the YouTuber for his money transfers, was Irish and it turns out that it's in fact the same account as the one used by Vassard, but with two different account numbers!"

A fist of steel suddenly clenched in Michael's gut. The conclusions would not be hard to draw, and the vice would close on the cult. And on him.

Pavlowski digested Pablo's statements and widened his eyes. "So we have four missing victims who lived in four different homes owned by the same real estate company, and now we see one identical beneficiary for their money. Find me the owner and the slightest element that could link them to The Children of Gaïa; I'll inform the DA right away to get a search warrant."

Just like in 1998, he thought, looking his teammate straight in the eye.

"Where are we with this key story?" Boris continued.

"We're still going through the comments under the post. Still nothing, but the news seems to have spread like wildfire," replied Patrick Fischer.

Satisfied, Boris nodded. "I also need someone on this S&M club, Gravity Zero."

He took a step back and spread his arms. Michael saw a facial tic that an inexperienced observer would not have seen: Boris had an idea in mind. "We're going to reshuffle the deck a bit here," he said. "Almeida and Fischer, you continue with your assignments, and try to get us as much information as possible about this bank account; you stay on the alert about the identification of the key. Alsayed, you will assist them, but you will focus on the cult. You get all the skeletons out of the closet! Monroe and King, as soon as this meeting is over, you're going to investigate Gravity Zero."

The young woman repressed a smile, but gave her friend a slight nudge under the table.

Michael should have been happy to finally be back with his much missed partner, but the idea that the staff of the nightclub could recognize him paralyzed him. At least he would be with Emma and, if the situation did not turn out to his advantage, she would be understanding.

A new black cloud had come to darken his day, and he felt an unpleasant sensation of unease. It was not like Boris to grant such favors; there was inevitably something behind this apparent complacency. He was going to be alone, free to conduct his own investigation, and this was not reassuring to Michael.

***

"Just like old times," Emma said as she got into the car.

Michael, who had rushed to open his door, hurried to grab his tube of painkillers and hastily put it in the glovebox.

"Hide your joy, Detective Monroe!" she said.

He turned towards her and gave her a genuine smile.

He was worried about Boris going it alone, but he couldn't fight the joy of being reunited with his long-term partner. Emma was smart and perceptive, and more importantly, she knew when to leave him alone and when to make conversation. She respected him as a person, and that, in his opinion, was her greatest quality.

As the car turned onto the avenue that bordered the parking lot, Emma entered the address of Gravity Zero into the GPS. Before she could start the navigation, Michael covered her hand with his and gently pushed it away from the screen.

"What are you doing?" she asked.

"We're not going there," he said brusquely.

"How come?"

"I have a better plan," he declared, feigning a smile.

He rummaged in his pocket and took out his cell phone, re-establishing his trajectory with a stroke of the wheel.

"Hey, watch the road!" she shouted.

"Go through my notes and enter the first address."

"What? *Dr. Louis Becker?*"

He nodded.

"In Canada?" she asked, frowning.

"Not quite," he replied, cryptically.

"Do you think I'm dumb? The red-and-white flag with a red maple leaf is Canada, right?"

"And yet, we're still staying on US soil."

"What's the deal? He built himself a house right on the border, his living room in the US and his bedroom in Canada?"

"Almost. You'll see."

Emma knew that tone of voice and that look: Michael would not answer any more questions. Sometimes she wondered if he was just being facetious or if he really knew what he was doing.

She took her smartphone out of her pocket and launched a word game. The hour that separated them from their destination would allow her to complete one or two puzzles.

On their left, the Niagara River stretched along the road, and they could see a few blocks of sparse houses in the green immensity of the grassy fields, which made up most of the scenery.

They crossed a metal bridge that linked the two countries, over a river bisected by the imaginary border.

Michael slowed down and turned left, steering the car onto a gravel road that led down to the riverbank. Below them, they could see Louis Becker's home, and Emma understood what her friend had meant.

A boat was moored along a concrete embankment. On the deck, a man in a thick navy-blue jacket was busy scrubbing the wooden slats that made up the floor, using a stiff brush mounted on the end of a telescopic broom.

The boat was not as long as the few barges that floated on the calm waters on either side of the river, but it was still a big enough dwelling for a couple, or even a small family.

"Dr. Becker?" Michael called out loudly enough to cover the sound of the wind.

The man with the shaggy hair and unkempt beard suddenly turned, and squinted at the two detectives. He dropped his broom and made a visor with his hand. "Who's asking?" he shouted, obviously disturbed from his work.

Out of habit, Michael never announced out loud that he was a cop coming for a courtesy call: he knew very well what kind of feelings the sole mention of the word could provoke.

Without answering, he walked towards the boat and Emma followed him, the gravel crunching under their every step. "We're from the Rochester Police Department," he said quietly. "We just have a few questions to ask you."

Becker's face shadowed and he crossed his arms, his shoulders slightly back. It didn't take a specialist of non-verbal language to figure out that they weren't welcome, but Michael did pick up a few signs that allowed him to build a quick profile of his character.

According to his file, Becker was a prominent psychiatrist who had helped advance medical research in his chosen field, and who had been honored by his peers on numerous occasions for his work. The doctor was obviously unaccustomed to being in a subordinate position, which Michael thought would make him uncomfortable. As a fine manipulator, Michael opted for the gentle method. "It is about one of your patients, a mere routine investigation. You don't have to accept our presence and we won't come on board unless you give us permission. You're the *Captain*," Michael added with a smile.

Louis Becker's face relaxed and he uncrossed his arms to show them a footbridge to the bow of the boat. "Hold on tight to the side rails, it's very slippery."

The two detectives complied and joined the shrink as he went into the cabin.

The interior was cozy and the varnished wood decoration made the place warm. A slight swell, perceptible only when other boats passed, made the hammer of the small bell above the entrance swing gently.

A table, the same brown as the paneled walls and ceiling, was half encircled by an angled bench dressed in pretty satin-like blue cushions.

"Take a seat, I'll make us some coffee," said Becker.

He bent his back and entered the adjoining room through a low, narrow doorway.

Emma looked around the living room, inwardly wondering if she could live in such a place. Meanwhile, Michael was already envious of their host's lifestyle, which suited his solitary nature perfectly.

A moment later, the doctor returned with a metal tray that held a French press coffee maker and three large cups decorated in a nautical theme.

"We are on a 1977 Super Van Craft that took me over eight

years to refurbish," he said proudly. "It's the only remnant of a somewhat messy divorce. Anyway, my ex-wife always hated this boat."

His very pleasant behavior contrasted with his sharp face and icy welcome, and Michael concluded that he must not have seen many people and was therefore quite happy to receive visitors. From what he could see, the rooms in the inner shell were clean and tidy, reflecting a meticulous demeanor and a strong sense of respect for others and himself.

Michael brought the cup up under his nose and inhaled the scent. The freshly ground coffee wafted gently into his nostrils and triggered an instantaneous sensation of pleasure.

He was careful not to compliment the Captain on his coffee, because he wanted to keep a slight edge on him, even though the conversation was going to be polite. Michael and Emma were the law, and they needed to remind him now and then.

"We have a Christopher Tremblay in custody who, according to his file, seems to have spent time in a psychiatric unit of which you were the director," Michael said, breaking the silence that had settled comfortably in between the lapping of the waves on the hull.

At the mention of the name, Louis Becker took another sip of the steaming liquid. An unconscious gesture to hide behind the truth and to gain time to prepare his answer. "The St. John's Hospital is one of my creations," he said calmly.

Michael picked up on the term. *Creation*. He described it as if he were an artist speaking of one of his works.

"I built this unit in the early 2000s; the prototype was very avant-garde, even for the time," Becker continued.

"What about Christopher Tremblay?" Michael asked.

"I remember him very well," the doctor replied, scratching his thick beard dotted with silver threads. "He was in the criminal ward – which no longer exists – for a few years. The medical team and I did a great job with him. But if you're here, I guess the limits of his therapy have just been set."

"For what reason do you think we booked him in?"

Becker took another sip of coffee. "He entered St. John's to serve a prison sentence following an unfortunate event. His paranoid delusions led him to attack passersby with a knife. I cannot say that he was completely cured when he left my unit, but I can assure you that with the combination of proper medication and follow-up, he should have remained harmless. I would be saddened to learn today that he has hurt someone again."

"That's what we would like to know," said Michael as Dr. Becker frowned.

"I'm afraid I don't understand."

Michael turned to Emma and waited for her approval. She closed her eyelids in silence. "He turned himself in for the murder of four people," the detective explained. "We are actively looking for the victims."

Usually, the details of an investigation are never revealed to those being questioned, which gives the authorities a head start. Michael felt that in this case, because it was so strange, that it would be useful to let the psychiatrist be in the know.

When their host realized that the facts were extremely serious, he looked genuinely sad, and in an almost inaudible whisper, he let out a curse word.

"The problem, Doctor," Michael continued, "is that we know almost nothing about him and time is running out. We still hope to find the potential victims alive, but there aren't many clues to go on."

Becker sank into the soft seat back. "Is he still in custody?" he asked.

"Yes," said Michael with a grim face. "We're nearing the end of the legal deadline, and in a few hours he'll be released."

"Tell me a little about him. What is he like, now? How is he behaving?"

"He's almost mute. He keeps chanting the same sentence: 'I killed them all'. Nothing more."

Becker frowned. "This is bizarre. Earlier, you said, 'You're the Captain', with emphasis on the last word. You were probably afraid that I would deny you access to my boat, so you used the nickname they used to call me back at St. John's. If you know it, I guess Christopher was not so mute after all."

Michael had just discovered a worthy opponent. As in a game of chess, the doctor had moved a piece forward and made an opening, but this was a trap whose degree of elaboration the detective had to determine. He remained silent, scrutinizing his every move.

Then Emma intervened. "What makes you say that we were afraid that you would deny us on board?"

"My dear lady..."

"Detective King," she said, cutting him off.

"Detective King," he continued without showing any sign of embarrassment, "I am a Canadian citizen and my address is also in this beautiful country. I'm assuming that your colleague here did his duty and knew, before coming, that the boat we are on was moored on the other bank of the Niagara River, on the US side. This is because the harbor where my boat is usually moored is undergoing some work to bring it up to standards. He also knows, as well as you I'm sure, that to conduct an investigation in Canada, he would have needed a warrant and the presence of the local authorities, but he thinks that the fact that I am currently in the US allows him a little freedom. Technically, he is in the wrong, thus I'm having you here of my own free will."

Emma glared at Michael. She hated it more than anything when her friend didn't put all his cards on the table. How did she look now? "Just tell us what you know about Christopher Tremblay," she said with a hardened tone. "I assume you know what obstruction of justice means?"

He raised his hands in surrender. "Don't shoot, Detective King! You're here. That means I'm willing to help you. Unfortunately, I can't really tell you anything more about Christopher. If you say that he repeats this sentence over and over again, then he is in the middle of a dementia crisis. He really didn't say anything else?"

Michael squinted. "No. That sentence was on a loop. The only other thing he mentioned was your nickname."

"Under what circumstances did he tell you that?" Becker asked.

"He was in the middle of a crisis, I guess," Michael replied.

"Did he seem to you to be in a paranoid fit?"

"You could put it that way, yes," the detective said, nodding.

"How did you find out who he was, if he didn't say anything besides the two elements you just told me?"

"We're the ones asking the questions here, Mr. Becker," Emma said with annoyance.

"Doctor Becker."

A heavy silence filled the cabin. A light drizzle sprinkled the many windows that framed the room. Michael felt his colleague stiffen when the psychiatrist answered, so he reached out again. "What year did your patient leave the St. John's unit?"

Louis Becker pretended to think, looking up and scratching his beard slowly. He was a bad liar.

"Mmmm... five years ago, I think," he replied.

"Did you see him again after he was released?"

"Not personally, no. My marriage was already on the fence and I left my position as director of the hospital shortly after he served his sentence. Christopher, however, was under a monitoring order and had to have a psychiatric evaluation every year."

Michael straightened up on the bench. "Who was supposed to do these evaluations? You?" he asked.

"No," he said, laughing. "I guess a judge appointed a psychiatric expert or something. I suggest you go to St. John's, they'll be better at this than I am. I can give you the contact information and let them know you're coming, if that can help."

The detective shook his head, looked down at the screen of his cell phone and suddenly stood up.

Taken aback at first, Emma eventually mimicked him.

"That won't be necessary, thank you," Michael concluded.

Dr. Becker stood up as well. "Good. Let me show you out then," he said. He passed his two visitors and climbed the flight of stairs that led to the deck. A gust of wind blew his hair around. He stepped aside to give free access to the small footbridge that connected the boat to the mainland.

Halfway between the harbor and Michael's car, Louis Becker hailed the two detectives. "I hope you find these people... alive!" His voice was lost in the distant tumult of the Niagara River.

"What got into you?" said Emma when her partner finally slammed the door of the car. "He was on the verge of spilling the beans and all of a sudden you got up and, poof! You put an end to the interview."

"We weren't going to learn anything from him anymore," Michael replied.

"Your mentalist powers told you this?" she said sardonically.

"We have bigger fish to fry."

"Oh yeah? Care to let me know?"

"The key," he answered, putting the car in reverse. "I just got a text from Pavlowski. They know what it opens."

22

His stomach had finally gotten the better of him. When all his colleagues had deserted the precinct, Boris took a break and went out for a bite to eat.

He had a pepperoni pizza that, at that moment, seemed to be the best in the world. He thought of Michael and his fad diet and almost felt sorry for him. He was missing out on life's delights such as cheese and meat. No wonder his complexion was pallid and he always looked depressed.

Boris took a sip of sparkling water and looked at his watch. He had to hurry if he wanted to be back at the station for the day's debriefing and the visit of the DA. If they had no more leads in their case, the latter would have a short interview with their suspect and he would be released.

Full at last, he left the joint, crossed the street and got into his car. He looked in vain for something to pick his teeth with in his glove compartment, then started the engine. The dashboard showed an outside temperature of 39°F.

With the next step of his investigation playing over and over in his mind, Boris drove twenty minutes to an isolated wooden house in a small city on the outskirts of Rochester. The chimney was belching out white smoke, and when he got out of his car, he immediately understood why. The air felt ice cold.

He walked to the front door, wiped his thick shoes on the old mat and rang the doorbell.

A man who was only an inch shorter than him opened the door. Despite his age, Pavlowski immediately noticed he was obviously still an active athlete, his muscular chest protruding under his gray sweater.

"Hello," said the man.

"Captain," Boris replied with a military salute. "Are you Henry Saget?"

"Yes, I am."

"I'm Sergeant Boris Pavlowski," he said, extending a friendly hand.

Henry took it, but did not move from the doorway.

"I'm with the Rochester PD," he continued, "and if you don't mind, I'd like to ask you a few questions about a case we're having some trouble with."

Henry's silver eyebrows furrowed. "I don't see how I can help you."

"My investigation has me looking at links to older cases you were in charge of at the time; I thought I'd save a lot of time by coming to talk to you directly."

Captain Saget's face did not relax, but he agreed to let his visitor in. He did not allow him access to the living room and preferred to keep to the hallway, which had a low table and two ottomans. Henry used the area for his reading time in the middle of winter, when the sun filled the room all afternoon. "Sit down," he said, pointing to one of the seats.

Boris obliged and his host sat down a few seconds later. He remained silent, waiting for the tall blond man to finally reveal the reason for his presence. "The facts go back more than twenty years," Boris began, clearing his throat. "It was in 1998."

Henry stiffened. The mention of that particular year resonated in him in a singular way, as if it had been etched into every cell of his body. He didn't know what this cop was about to say, but he had a feeling he wouldn't like what he was going to hear.

"You see," Lieutenant Pavlowski continued, "we have a strange individual in custody who gave us a list of four people whom he claims to have murdered. We found on him a sort of business card that referred to a cult called The Children of Gaïa."

The old man jumped inwardly, but didn't let on that he knew the other man was studying his every move.

Boris paused for a moment and then continued, "The reason I came here today is simple. I discovered a report about an old case in the archives of the Rochester PD, a case in which you and your team carried out a search on the property of this cult. I found the report to be a bit stingy on the details, but I guess that was the way back in the old days."

"What do you mean by a 'bit stingy on the details'?" asked Henry in as neutral a tone as possible.

"Let's just say that I feel like there are some important facts missing... Do you have anything to drink? I think the meal I just had was way too salty."

Surprised by the sudden request, Saget stood up and offered the lieutenant a glass of water, which he gladly accepted. This short truce allowed him to regain his composure and collect himself. He did not appreciate the way this discussion was going. The past was not meant to be stirred up.

When he returned to the room, Boris was standing with his hands crossed behind his back, looking at the framed pictures displayed on an oak chest of drawers. Henry handed him the glass and sat back down.

"Thank you very much," said Boris, sitting down.

With the slowness of those who are in control of the situation, the visitor took two long sips and put the glass back on the table in front of him.

"As I said," Boris continued, "the man we have in custody doesn't want to talk, and if we don't find conclusive evidence, he will be released and we won't have made much progress. We believe that the victims he mentioned may still be alive. Time is running out."

"I hear what you're saying, but I don't see how I can help you. I'm sorry," Henry replied.

"Do you know Detective Michael Monroe?"

The word was out. Saget would have bet everything he had that this too-polite-to-be-honest investigator had come to confront him about Michael.

He swallowed, then loosened his jaw, his face still impassive. "Of course," said Henry. "He was under my command for almost ten years."

"Good," Boris replied calmly. "I've read and reread the report on that famous search of The Children of Gaïa estate, and there's something that's bothering me. I know he lived among the cult as a teenager, but his name isn't mentioned anywhere, and his parents and sister were questioned."

The old man remained inscrutable. His chess player's mind was analyzing the moves made by his interlocutor. The former captain had made sure to cover his tracks and lock up all traces of The Children of Gaïa before his retirement. He made sure to secure them with the highest degree of confidentiality, and as few officers as possible would have access to them. He nevertheless wondered if this lieutenant would have been allowed access to these most sensitive of reports.

Henry had no idea how his host could have obtained this information, and it seemed to him that he was telling a lie to get at the truth. "It's an old case," he finally replied, "and we've interviewed over fifty people. My recollection of the events is not very reliable."

"You did know Detective Monroe had been a member of the cult, right?"

The condescending tone of Boris began to get on his nerves, but he remained stoic. "Yes, I knew about it," Henry replied.

"But don't you remember why he wasn't present during the search in 1998?"

"You know, this cult has grounds and establishments all over the US and even abroad. They have their own methods and send their followers on retreats out in the country so that they can be alone with themselves and get closer to God. It's possible that on this very day, Michael Monroe, and many others, were removed from the estate."

"It's possible, yes," Pavlowski said with a frown. He paused, staring straight into Saget's eyes. The former captain's blood was starting to boil, but he didn't let it show.

After a long minute, he stood up and clasped his hands together. "Well," Henry concluded, "if you don't have any more questions, I have a busy evening ahead of me. I'm sorry I wasn't able to help you, but if my memory comes back, I'll be sure to let you know."

Boris stood up and reached into one of his jacket pockets. "If you need to reach me," he said, handing him a business card.

"I'll call the station, don't worry," said the old man, declining the object.

Boris bent down and put the card on the table, next to his glass of water, in a gesture that had everything to do with defiance.

Saget opened the door and let the cold in.

His visitor walked outside, then stopped. "Mary Saget, does that mean anything to you?" Boris whispered to him.

Flames of hatred ignited Henry's eyes, and he contracted his jaw muscles. He gave the unwanted guest a few seconds to get out but as Boris remained motionless in the doorway, obviously waiting for a reaction from Henry, he lost his temper.

He stretched out his arm so quickly that Pavlowski didn't see it coming. The powerful hand of Henry was already gripping Boris's throat.

He threw him to the left and dragged him against the adjacent wall. The effect of surprise gave him the upper hand in a fight which, without that, would have been to the advantage of the younger of the two. Saget transferred all his weight forward, compressing his opponent's windpipe. He brought his mouth to his bloated face. "Listen to me, asshole," Henry spat, "I've got nearly forty years on the job, I've led the department you're in, and with a snap of my fingers, I can transfer you to a shithole where you'll be lucky if you investigate on cases of roadkill. What you are looking for is not to be found where you've been rummaging around. Forget about that lead and focus on something else."

He released his grip and stepped back, his eyes bloodshot. Boris could finally breathe, and he inhaled deeply. He wiped a stream of saliva from the corner of his mouth with his clenched fist and left the house under Henry's murderous gaze.

From inside his car, he heard the door slam. He tilted the rearview mirror to check his reflection and massaged his neck. He reached into one of his jacket pockets and pulled out a crumpled-looking photograph, which he tossed onto the passenger seat.

In the picture, Henry Saget, thirty years younger, was embracing a smiling young woman who was holding a child by the hand. The boy must have been barely two years old, and despite the decades that separated him from the time the photo was taken, Pavlowski had no trouble recognizing Michael. The resemblance between Mary Saget and Henry was also clear: they were siblings.

Michael and Emma rushed into the open space, swinging open the two doors and scattering a small pile of papers out of the nearest office.

The two detectives spotted a small crowd around Fischer's workstation and joined in.

"So?" asked Michael.

Patrick Fischer pointed to his computer screen. "Someone found something," he said.

"What?"

"The inscriptions etched on the key are not a coat of arms," said Patrick. "But rather the base of a lighthouse and a date: 1822. The person who gave us the information is a teenager whose father rents a storage unit near the Charlotte-Genesee Lighthouse. You all recognize this landmark, right?"

Everyone nodded in agreement. That building sided with an octagonal tower was well known among the Rochester community and kids from schools all around the county visited it throughout the year.

Alsayed held up the clear plastic bag containing the key and pointed to the partial date indicating the year the lighthouse was built.

Michael looked around the room and frowned. "Where's Boris?" he asked.

Fischer and Almeida shrugged.

"He went out for a bite to eat, I think," Jamal said. "He hasn't come back yet."

A new knot of worry formed in the detective's stomach. The

idea that his superior might end up conducting an investigation without him was troubling.

"It doesn't matter," Emma said.

"According to my research, there was a big warehouse next to the lighthouse building that was recently converted into storage spaces. I think the organization in charge was looking for funds for annual maintenance and restoration. They came up with this solution a few years ago."

"What are we waiting for?" Michael asked in an almost hysterical tone. "Let's go out there!"

"We were waiting for orders," Fischer said as an excuse.

Michael moved away from the circle formed by the other officers and hurried towards Assia's office. He knocked frantically on the door and, a few seconds later, she allowed him to enter.

When she saw her lover's face appear, a brief shiver tickled her neck. Contradictory feelings intermingled: his attitude since they were brought back together the day before was irritating her, but she couldn't forget that the whole precinct was busy on an important case and that their love affair should not interfere with it.

The tense look on Michael's face seemed to indicate that there was something new, so she pushed back her thoughts and she listened carefully.

"Captain, we have found the origin of the key that Tremblay swallowed, and we would like permission to go there urgently," Michael said in a formal tone.

Assia frowned. "Isn't Lieutenant Pavlowski there with you?"

"Negative."

"Go ahead then. I'll try to reach him," she said, picking up the landline phone in front of her.

"Before that, we need to send the paramedics to the Charlotte-Genesse Lighthouse right away."

"What?" she asked, her mouth agape with astonishment.

"The key opens a storage space in a warehouse next to it: our four victims may be inside," said Michael.

Assia's eyes widened. She hung up and picked up the receiver again to call 911.

23

———

A van, painted in the colors of the Rochester PD, was waiting for Michael outside the precinct exit. Fischer was behind the wheel, Emma was in the passenger seat, and Almeida was in the back, leaning with difficulty to the side to open the sliding door for his colleague.

Michael jumped in and Fischer stepped on the gas. As soon as they were out of the parking lot, Emma put on the flashing lights, and the small team of investigators sped dangerously toward their destination, running red lights.

Michael grabbed his cell phone and dialed Boris's number. After two rings, he picked up. "Where are you?" Michael asked without waiting for an answer. "We're heading for the Charlotte-Genesee Lighthouse. The key most certainly opens a storage space there."

"I'm on my way," said Pavlowski.

Michael hung up. Next to him, Almeida was staring at him as if he were studying an animal in a zoo. "What's wrong?" he asked.

Michael's forehead was beaded with sweat and his heart was

beating much too fast. With each turn, he felt dizzy and swallowed hard to keep from vomiting. The pills he had been gulping down at high frequency since the previous day did not mix well with undernourishment and a lack of carbohydrates. The fear of arriving too late that was taking hold of the detective in successive waves did not help. The idea of finding four dead bodies in this storage unit was causing him to have a panic attack.

The engine was roaring, Fischer zigzagging amongst the cars, and the traffic finally thinned out to let them through. It took them more than fifteen minutes to reach the lighthouse landmark, whose tower rose into the air, seeming to defy them with its height.

Emma pointed to an old warehouse next to it that must have once housed boats or naval gear. A modern-looking sign indicated the storage units and a telephone number in blue letters that clashed with the ancient beauty of the old stones.

The van turned right onto a paved road and approached the large wooden door that marked the entrance. A central aisle distributed twelve spaces: six on either side.

At the back, two men were unloading a pickup truck, barely disturbed by the noisy arrival of the Rochester police.

Michael jumped out of the vehicle and ran with short strides to the first stall. He knocked violently and repeatedly on the heavy wooden door. The sound echoed throughout the building like the tolling of a bell tower. "Rochester PD!" he shouted.

While Fischer was trying the key, Michael went to the opposite side and repeated his summons. The two employees in the background stopped their activity and looked confused. Emma was already walking over to meet them to take preliminary statements.

The third storage space, which looked much newer, had a

metal door and a modern lock that obviously didn't match their key, which didn't work in the lock of the fourth unit either.

Michael's blood seemed to thicken and he felt heavier and heavier, as if gravity was intensifying as he moved deeper into the building. His senses were on high alert, and he was listening for any sign of the presence of Christopher Tremblay's victims.

Fischer stuck the big key in the lock of stall number five, and the metallic clanking that followed was greeted by the sighs of relief of the officers. They crowded around him and Michael drew his gun.

He nodded to Patrick in the eerie silence.

The door opened onto a room devoid of light, and the smell that emanated from inside jumped to Michael's nostrils. It was a mixture of varnished wood, dirt, and dust.

Emma pulled the SIG Sauer from its holster with one hand and held up a flashlight with the other. She looked at Michael and nodded.

Arms stretched forward and legs slightly bent, he slowly entered the storage room, each step guided by his colleague's flashlight.

A circle of white light illuminated an indistinct cluster at the back of the room.

Michael crossed his left arm under his right and felt around with his hand on the nearest wall. His fingertips touched a plastic protrusion, whose function he immediately identified.

Four long neon lights on the ceiling lit up with characteristic crackles. One of them flashed for a few seconds and then stabilized.

Under the scrutiny of a surgical white light, the storage room finally revealed its contents to the investigators. A third of the space was occupied by a chest-high pile of objects. Several dusty tarpaulins of different colors served to hide what was underneath.

The image of Christopher Tremblay troubled Michael's mind in successive flashes. He remembered his emaciated, beardless face, his dark, impenetrable eyes and his blood-curdling coldness. This unbalanced man had taken the risk of swallowing a big metal key to try and hide this room from the police. Why?

Michael hoped to get the beginning of an answer. Perhaps the truth lay beneath these old tarps. He grabbed a corner and pulled.

A cloud of dust rose up, and when it dissipated, they all realized what they were looking at.

Furniture; tables and chairs, a desk and musical instruments. Two guitar cases were leaning against the wall, a long keyboard with yellowed keys was gathering dust on a modern-looking white dresser. Cables and microphones in their boxes filled the three bulky drawers.

Annoyed, Michael pulled another tarp and discovered an upright bass, several speakers and a mixing desk, lying carelessly to one side.

He crouched down and looked around at the rest of the objects piled up at the back of the room. A tangle of chairs, coatracks and wooden planks that made no sense to him or to the police officers around him.

Why on earth had their suspect taken care to hide this place from them?

Screeching tires in the driveway announced the arrival of Boris Pavlowski.

Irritated, Michael left the storage room and let his colleagues collect the first clues.

"So?" said Boris to him as he got out of his car.

"Nothing," Michael replied, shaking his head nervously.

His superior approached him with large strides. "What do you mean?" he asked.

"Nothing special. Just furniture, musical instruments, chairs... nothing," Michael concluded.

Boris noticed that he was clenching his fist; he gave the impression that he was greatly affected by this news. A little too much, perhaps. "Musical instruments? Is it possible that this stuff belongs to... what was his name?"

"Sheepmann," Michael replied.

"Yes, that's it. That would explain why his apartment was almost empty."

Detective Monroe raised his eyebrows and looked surprised. He didn't really see what Boris was getting at. "So what? Tremblay kills Sheepmann, moves all his belongings here and swallows the key?"

"Why not?" replied Pavlowski. "The answer has to be in this storage room."

He was probably right but, disappointed, Michael seemed suddenly detached from the investigation. His greatest hope had been to find the four victims alive in this squalid, dusty room. His greatest fear had been to find himself confronted with four corpses; but at the end of this dark hypothesis, Christopher Tremblay would have been cornered and it wouldn't have been long before the murders could be pinned on him. But Boris was right, they discovered what that key opened and, even if it seemed to Michael that the room offered only meager clues, there was inevitably something inside that their suspect wanted to hide from the investigators.

He pulled himself together and rejoined his colleagues, grabbing a pair of blue latex gloves out of a plastic crate Almeida had brought near the entrance of the warehouse.

Inside the room, Emma had scattered the contents about her to inspect them more closely. Pavlowski looked at each item in detail, and Michael was already opening the drawers and emptying the few cupboards before the Crime Scene technicians arrived.

After a few minutes, he examined a small white bathroom cabinet and found a shoebox inside, which he quickly grabbed.

He placed it on the floor, squatted down and lifted the lid. He discovered a rectangular mass wrapped in aluminum foil, the size of a small brick.

Intrigued, he removed the metallic wrapping and revealed to everyone four cell phones of the same model, stacked on top of each other and held together by a thick rubber band.

"Bingo!" said Emma, almost taking the words out of Michael's mouth.

The sun had lost its battle against the impenetrable blanket of clouds, and the light was inexorably declining. As dusk approached, the temperature was giving up a few degrees as well.

Back at the precinct, Assia had installed the technicians and their equipment in the largest interrogation room. The two young men had taken over the room in no time.

Their screens bathed the room in a bluish light, while their computers hummed softly, waiting to be fed data for decryption. Anticipating the processing time of such an undertaking, the two tech guys had the foresight to bring a coffee machine with them, which they quickly put into use.

One of them, wearing antistatic gloves, grabbed one of the cell phones found in the storage room and plugged it in. His colleague followed suit and, each in front of their screen, they launched a high-performance decryption program with the aim of unlocking the SIM cards.

After each attempt, the program forced the smartphones'

cache memory to reset, so that they would believe that each new attempt at the PIN code was the first. The machine had to repeat the operation a maximum of 9,998 times, and that was it. The whole thing ran with the speed of electrons in a computer system, but what surprised the two agents was that the very first attempt was the right one.

No sooner had they run the software than a small crystalline sound signaled that the unlocking key had been found: 0000.

The technicians turned to each other and smiled in silence.

The taller one stood up and turned on the two remaining phones. Without even plugging them into his computer, he entered the four-digit series, and he instantly unlocked the phones.

Most people don't take the time to change their PIN code, and use the original one. The second most common set of numbers is 1234 and their program was set up to test these two common combinations on the first try.

Each device's memory was flashed and copied entirely to their hard drives. An emulator software allowed them to navigate the screens as if they were actually using the phones.

First check: the call log. The two cyber-investigators were immediately struck by a singular occurrence of an identical phone number on all four devices on the same day, a few hours earlier. One of the technicians noted the information and continued to search the memory of the smartphones. There were no pictures and very few numbers in the contacts.

With so few leads, they felt their work was coming to an end, so they decided to call their fellow officers and give them their initial findings.

Boris entered the room first, followed by Michael, Emma and Jamal. The squad was almost complete: only Fischer and Almeida had remained at the lighthouse warehouse with the Crime Scene agents.

The young technician waited until all the officers were settled around his screen and made sure that everyone could see it. "Here's what we've got so far," he said. "First and foremost, the same phone number contacted these four cell phones in quick succession. 3:37pm for the first, 3:38pm for the second and third, and finally 3:39pm for the last."

"Do we know who called?" asked Michael.

"The number isn't saved in any of the terminals."

"If someone was trying to reach these four phones at the same moment, they must have known their owners," Michael concluded.

"Here's the phone number used to contact them," the agent said, handing out a piece of paper. "Strangely enough," he continued, "there are no pictures and almost no entries in the directories. We'll keep digging for a few hours to see if there are any hidden or encrypted files somewhere in the memory, but for now, that's about all we have."

"Can we find out who the phones belong to?" asked Emma.

"The SIM cards are prepaid subscriptions."

"Burners," whispered Michael, before walking over to the desk and pointing to something on the monitor. "Those are their phone screens right there?"

"Right. We copied all the data and this software simulates browsing the phones."

"On this home screen here," the detective said, taking a step forward, "you can click on the apps?"

"Absolutely."

Michael brought his index finger to a red icon that

represented a simplified graph, with a curve that drew dips and peaks.

"Click here, please."

The technician obliged, and a folder with new applications opened.

"Look, these are stock market apps. I bet this phone belongs to Colin Vassard, the trader," said Michael.

Emma and Boris suddenly seemed much more interested and leaned toward the screen.

"Can we see the others, please?" asked Michael, whose excitement was gradually building.

In response, the technician laid out the copied image of the three remaining devices across the entirety of his monitor's space.

Michael looked around at the various colored icons lined up before his eyes and stopped on one of them. "There!" he shouted. "The Twitch app! That's the video platform Slevin Bradich uses to broadcast his content."

The cyber-investigator allowed himself a remark. "And there's an app to do video editing on a smartphone."

"All right," Emma said suddenly, "we can assume that this one belongs to Bradich. What do the other two say?"

"Not much, in my opinion, we'll need to get the itemized bill and triangulate the devices' signals," said Michael. "I just wanted confirmation that these phones belonged to the victims we're looking for."

"This ain't good," Boris huffed.

"What do you mean?" Michael asked.

"We were all hoping to find our four missing people alive in that storage unit... but now it's back to square one. We don't even have any bodies."

"This just raises the hope that they are still alive! Let's identify the owners of all the phone numbers we have, especially the one that called the four cell phones this afternoon."

One of the two agents intervened. "The area code says it's a Canadian number, if that's any indication."

Suddenly, Michael stiffened. He took one last look at the digits, mentally recorded them, and abruptly left the room.

24

In the open space, the police officers were glancing at their watches, a sign that the day was stretching out a little too far for their liking. Outside, the thick night had covered the mountains in the distance, like a wave of noxious oil.

All the phone numbers had been sent to be checked, but given the late hour, the results would not come in until the next morning, at best. Not soon enough to prevent Christopher Tremblay from being released.

Emma returned to her desk and looked at the piles of papers in front of her. She decided to do some tidying up so she could have the satisfaction of starting the day ahead with a clean desk. She sorted through her notes, put the chewed-up pens back in their jar, and suddenly lingered over a photocopy of the list written by their suspect.

She sat down, placed the sheet of paper in front of her, and concentrated on the four clumsily scrawled names. Something had been nagging at her all along, but she hadn't had a chance to give her intuition time.

Michael approached her and saw her massaging her temples. "Are you meditating?" he asked.

Emma shook her head and looked up at her colleague. "Something is bothering me," she admitted.

"What, on this list?"

"Yes, I still can't get used to the way the names are spelled. Tod with one D, Sheepmann with two Ns..."

"At first, I was like you. I thought our guy had made spelling mistakes; but no, even on his statement, that's how it's written."

"The fact that Tod Sheepmann is an artist makes me wonder. I have the vague impression that it's a pseudonym."

"Possible. Composers often do that," Michael conceded.

"If it's a pseudonym, he must have had a reason for this odd spelling."

"You're the word puzzle expert," he said, pointing to the book that sat atop her pile of papers.

"Could it be..." she whispered, not paying attention to her friend anymore.

She grabbed a pen and a blank sheet of paper, and wrote the name, in well-spaced capital letters.

TODCSHEEPMANN

Accustomed to solving anagrams, she used a method that had taken her years to perfect. After about ten minutes and two completely crossed-out sheets, she decided to start over on a blank page.

She squinted and moved her face away from the text, as if to take a step back from the puzzle. It seemed to her that the letters nevertheless evoked something, something to do with music. Where had she seen a similar term before?

She then opened her internet browser and went to one of the crossword sites she often used. In the empty field waiting for a definition, she typed "composer". A list of possibilities sorted by the number of letters appeared as soon as she validated her request. She looked at it several times, but it didn't give her anything conclusive.

Suddenly, a small glimmer of light came to life in the back of her mind. She opened her search engine and wrote, "Canadian composer". When she pressed *return* on her keyboard, a slight tingling sensation ran down the back of her neck.

Running across the width of the page, portraits of musicians lined up in a sort of speckled banner. She scrolled to the right, and this time, an intense shiver ran through her body. At the sight of one of the names, her eyes widened and she rushed for her pen.

Stephen Codman, a composer born in England who came to Canada in 1816. A distant memory resurfaced. When she was still a schoolgirl, she had joined a choir, at the suggestion of her music teacher. The only reason she had agreed to sacrifice all her Wednesday evenings for half the year was that Olivia, a girl whose beauty fascinated her and whose attraction to her she could not explain at the time, was also participating. Among the pieces the choir members had been rehearsing for six months was one by Stephen Codman.

She felt the same kind of excitement that used to seize her when she was about to solve a word puzzle that she had been working on for hours.

Doing the reverse maneuver, she wrote the composer's name in capital letters and worked to reconstruct Tod C. Sheepmann's full name with all the letters. Everything matched perfectly. *Bingo!*

As a small group of officers at the back of the room were on their way out and Boris himself was about to grab his heavy jacket, she declared to the crowd, "I've got something!"

Michael was the first to turn around. He recognized the distinctive, high-pitched tone his partner used when she'd hooked a lead. Pavlowski followed suit a few seconds later. Like wolves tracking prey, the two men moved with hushed steps, as if they were afraid of losing the trail their colleague had just discovered.

Finally, when they reached Emma's desk, they bent over dozens of scribbled sheets of paper, but at the bottom of one of them, two words had been circled in a hurried and victorious manner.

"Tod C. Sheepmann is the anagram of Stephen Codman!" she said, capturing the attention of the entire assembly. The perplexed faces around her asked her to specify. "He's a Canadian composer!"

Eager to test her theory, she looked again at the list of names. Instinctively, she chose the one she thought would be the easiest to decode. Slevin B. Bradich. Indeed, the videographer's name seemed easier to fiddle with.

Before the astonished eyes of her teammates, Emma repeated the operation. She spread out the letters of the victim's name:

S L E V I N B B R A D I C H

As one hunch led to another, she typed "biggest Twitch streamers" into the search engine, and when she saw the results come up, her heart raced. At the top of the list of about twenty names, her eyes were immediately drawn to the first one.

She quickly arranged the letters and was able to form the first name Bradich, after which she found herself with a remnant of seven letters – S, L, E, V, I, N and B – which obviously made up the last name "Blevins". Bradich Blevins. AKA Ninja on his Twitch channel dedicated to the video game Fortnite. That name was well known in the gamer community. He was the most famous and the most followed streamer on the platform.

"Shall I continue?" Emma proudly asked the two policemen. They nodded in silence and the beautiful redhead went on. "We still have Jenni Grosch-Steiner and Colin Vassard."

"Do a search for 'famous trader' on Google," Michael said, a hint of excitement in his voice.

She typed it in the search bar.

Amidst the Frenchman Jerome Kerviel, Tom Hayes, and Warren Buffett, a link led to an article listing the top ten traders of all time. Emma kept the less common letters in mind, such as C and V, and looked at all the names in the list with an expert eye. One caught her attention, the author of a book with the unmistakable title, *How I Made $2,000,000 in the Stock Market*: Nicolas Darvas.

She quickly reconstructed the anagram, but one character was too many: the A. This struck her as odd. "It's weird," she said, frowning.

"What?" said Boris, almost tense.

"I have one too many A's..."

"Is it that important?" he asked.

"There's no point in making an anagram of someone's name if you're going to omit or add letters. It doesn't make any sense," Emma replied.

Michael sat up, as if jolted by an electric shock.

"I know!" he thundered. "The plates on his mailbox and on his door read: Colin A. Vassard! There's your A!"

Emma smiled brightly back at him. "I'm coming to get you, Jenni!" she said cheerfully. Then she turned her gaze to her screen and froze, as if paralyzed by an unknown evil.

"What is it?" Michael asked.

"How am I supposed to do this? Searching for 'most famous prostitutes'? Come on!" she answered, shaking her head.

Michael squinted and paused. "Try 'famous transsexuals'!" he said.

Slightly doubtful, she launched the search.

The first result was a very serious feature article about transgender people who have made history. Some of the stories went back three hundred and fifty years, such as the French Abbot of Choisy who became Madame de Sancy in 1672. Boris and Michael followed the information on the screen with their eyes as the young woman scrolled through the text. She ignored other anecdotes dating back to the French kings, then the one about the life of a showgirl in Paris during the Roaring Twenties, and finally came across the very first person in the world to have undergone sex reassignment surgery. An American actress born in the 1920s named Christine Jorgensen.

The young woman did a quick calculation: eighteen letters in both names. According to her, no coincidence was possible, and with impressive vivacity, she verified that Jenni Grosch-Steiner was indeed the anagram of the famous New Yorker. "It's a match," Emma said.

"Impressive," Michael replied, congratulating her, without any real conviction in his tone of voice.

"What's wrong?" she asked, sensing his disappointment.

"Nothing," he replied. "You did a great job, Emma, but where's the real progress in this case? These anagrams only prove that the true identity of the victims is once again hidden from us."

"You're right," she said. "We just know that all the names on this list are fake... At the end of the day, it just pushes us a little farther away from the truth."

"On the contrary!" shouted Boris. "It confirms our most reliable lead: the cult. Good job, Emma."

Michael shrugged and frowned. "I don't think it confirms anything," he grumbled.

"What do you make of The Children of Gaïa and their methods? It's a perfect match. We've got offshore bank accounts, the fake IDs, and then the disappearance of the members into thin air. It's exactly the same MO, and thanks to Emma's efforts, we're even closer to the truth."

"Christopher Tremblay confessed to killing those four people, remember?" said Michael.

"Our suspect was carrying a business card with The Children of Gaïa logo on it, and I didn't think for a second that there was another side to the story besides this one," Boris replied.

"There were never any murder cases linked to the cult," Michael said with a grimace.

"Until now."

"Why would this guy kill cult members and then come forward to confess his crimes? It doesn't make any sense."

"It's up to us to find out," Pavlowski said. "Did he follow the orders of the cult or did he act against it?"

Michael moved away from his two colleagues, his face dark. "Let's see what the phone numbers tell us before we jump to any conclusions," he said.

Why does he keep on defending the people who have broken his childhood and family ties? Boris wondered.

25

"See you tomorrow, Emma," Michael said, waving to his colleague, "and good job on the anagrams!"

He grabbed his jacket and headed for the exit. On the way, he checked his cell phone. No new messages.

It had been a long day, and at the thought of going home and being alone, a knot of anxiety began to grow in his gut again. To cheer himself up, he reread Assia's text message and decided to discreetly pass by her office before leaving.

The door was ajar and he took a furtive look inside. Completely empty. A little disappointed, he scanned the surroundings with a circular glance, but no trace of the boss of the Rochester PD. Not wanting to raise the slightest suspicion about their relationship, he didn't dare ask if anyone knew where she was.

He clenched his fists and left the station to find himself in the middle of a freezing rain shower, which assailed him with thousands of tiny daggers already piercing the first layers of his clothes.

He ran to his car and threw himself inside. A cloud of steam came out of his mouth as he exhaled loudly. He caught his breath for a moment and considered his options.

First, Michael pulled out his smartphone and quickly typed in the Canadian phone number that the technicians had found on the various cell phones. He contemplated the digits on his lighted screen for a few seconds, then tossed the device onto the passenger seat. This was not the time to do something stupid. He had already suffered from this kind of behavior in the past. It was true that in the absence of new evidence or bodies, their suspect would be released; but he suppressed the urge to call. The investigation would have to follow official protocol.

The rain was getting heavier as he got closer to his home, and his windshield wipers were no longer fast enough to provide good visibility. Naturally cautious, Michael eased up on the gas pedal and focused his attention on the road.

Reflecting the darkness of the clouds, the lake had taken on a charcoal hue, as if it were composed of liquid onyx. A flare of lightning struck the crest of a hill in the distance and seemed to freeze the scene, like a photographer's flash.

The small road he was now taking rose above the valley on his left and led him through rows of trees whose leaves covered the asphalt, swiped by successive gusts of wind.

It was getting darker at the edge of the forest, and the beam of his headlights struggled to pierce the thick curtain of rain.

As he approached his home, he slowed down. The ground-floor windows diffused soft light from the living room and his landlady's kitchen. With this kind of weather, she would surely deviate from her daily ritual of peppering Michael with questions as soon as he popped out of his car and approached the house.

When he unlocked his front door, he was surprised to hear meowing. Two cats, a brown-striped tabby and an overweight ginger, rubbed their furry cheeks against his legs, and he concluded that the two felines had been caught in the rain. The cat flap he'd installed – after his landlady had reluctantly agreed – had allowed them to take shelter and eat the few kibbles he always left available for them.

No sooner had he filled two bowls of food than the doorbell rang.

She couldn't resist, he told himself, thinking he would soon be disturbed by his landlady.

But when he opened the door, he found Assia's perfect figure peeking through the rain. His heart leaped and he was stunned for a few seconds. "Can I come in? I'm soaked," she said.

He stammered an inaudible answer and moved aside to let her in. Torn between the apprehension of having allowed Assia to invade his cocoon without being prepared and the joy of meeting again, he remained silent for several long seconds.

"I didn't know that you had cats," she said finally.

"I... They're not mine," he replied shyly.

"You're some kind of cat-sitter?"

Michael's black eyebrows now formed an elongated V. "Uh... no, they're the neighborhood cats. They come and go, I give them food, they wake me up at dawn, you know the drill," he answered, with a smile, one of the few that wasn't fake.

"Will you show me around?"

A little disconcerted, Michael complied, trying to be as natural a guide as possible. He took a few steps and made a circle with his arms. "So, this is the living room with, as you can see, an open kitchen."

She crossed the room to approach the bay window at the back, which took up the entire width.

The view was breathtaking. The apartment overlooked the

valley that descended to the lake and behind it, in the distance, the hills cut through the earth to impose themselves as guardians of these immemorial waters. The rain made the leaves of the trees glow, illuminated by the halos of the streetlamps at the edge of the road.

"Not a bad view," noted Assia with a small admiring pout. She turned and waited for the tour to resume.

"Upstairs, there's the bedroom and bathroom."

"I'll follow you," she said, her voice slightly huskier.

They climbed the stairs and came to an attic room that Michael had decorated with taste, and whose various light sources, diffusing a soft and warm glow, made it very cozy. Raindrops pounded on the roof and skylights, and Assia had the sudden urge to snuggle with her man under the blanket.

She looked around and saw a telescope in a corner and, in a sort of alcove on the left, a lotus flower mat and an incense holder with a half-burned stick pointing at it. She frowned slightly and could not help but remark, "Is this your meditation corner?"

"You could say that," Michael replied, still a little uncomfortable.

Assia took a step towards him and removed her soaked jacket that she let carelessly fall on the ground. She stepped forward again and placed her lips on those of her lover. He closed his eyes and embraced her.

They did not even make time to undress completely and fell down on the bed. Assia felt a slight restraint in Michael's gestures, and she set about breaking down his last barriers by adopting a more lascivious attitude, not hesitating to encourage him to take the lead in giving her pleasure.

"Thank you for welcoming me into your home," she said as a shiver ran through her body. "I know that I forced you a little, but you have to admit that you're not the easiest to read."

"Are you cold?" Michael asked.

"A little."

Michael pulled the quilt over them. He drew close to snuggle against her. Assia savored every second of this moment as if it were her last. She turned on her side and their two half-naked bodies fitted together like two pieces of a matching set.

"Can we talk a bit?" she asked him.

She felt him tense up. Michael took a deep breath. "Okay," he conceded, "but about anything except the case."

He heard the sheets crease and he figured Assia nodded. "Two months ago, your burnout," she said, "what was the real reason?"

She knew that it was a shot in the dark, and faced with the slightest annoyance, a complex man like Michael was capable of shutting down for a long time, and becoming impervious to any feeling. As cold as a stone.

He freed his hand from Assia's and turned onto his back, his eyes lost in the darkness of the room. The weight of the secret was now too heavy and he allowed himself to share it with her. "Your typical cop story, I guess," he said with a sigh.

She groped for the warmth of her man's body and put her palm on his thigh. She caressed it gently.

"I had a young girl in for a complaint of sexual assault. She knew her attacker: it was the janitor of her building. As you can imagine, she was terrified and, unfortunately, she had taken too long to come to us: the events were in fact several months old. We did the checks and the guy had an alibi for the day of the assault. It was killing me that I couldn't follow up on the complaint, so I interviewed the victim again. I knew that her mind was foggy and that, almost six months later, she could have been wrong by a day or two. But she seemed to be positive about the date. For her, it was indeed a Saturday, as she didn't have school, and the man had attacked her in the basement, in the parking space where she was about to take her bike to go to a friend's house. Her non-verbal language told me that there was something more. She was ashamed, she didn't dare reveal anything to me. I was able to get her to trust me and she finally opened up. Her attacker had kept her panties. She was so scared that she'd gone on as usual, as if nothing had happened, burying this secret deep inside her. She hadn't dared to tell me this detail, because she'd been without her underwear all day and, in retrospect, she found it humiliating." Michael paused. The sound of the two lovers breathing was covered by the rain pelting on the roof tiles.

"The janitor had already made his statement," Michael continued, "and his alibi checked out. I would never have been able to get a search warrant for his house. So... I went there... One Sunday, while he had gone to the movies with his wife, I broke into his house. I searched everything, from top to bottom. There was a room, a sort of laundry room, which had been converted into a simple office with a computer and a printer, and when I went in, I had an intuition. In the double bottom of one of the drawers in the cabinet, I found four pairs of panties."

Assia turned around and hugged him.

"I was mad with rage and made the mistake of letting anger get the better of me. I... I waited for this guy to come back home and I collared him in front of his wife and a brawl ensued. On Monday morning, at the precinct, I went to see Captain Saget and told him how I had become sure that this son of a bitch had assaulted at least three other victims. He told me that I had been reckless in doing this and that my last hope was to call the janitor back for an interview, and pray that he would confess without mentioning my break-in at his house. I called him back within a week and he showed up with a lawyer. I found myself between a rock and a hard place. If the case went to court, the guy would immediately press charges against me, and we all know how that would have ended."

"Abuse of power, tampering with evidence, and the guy walking free after a dismissal," said Assia, her face buried in Michael's shoulder.

"And as far as I'm concerned, administrative sanctions, maybe worse... Anyway, we just dropped it. We turned a blind eye to it all and everyone went home. I couldn't go on with my day as if nothing had happened, and I flipped out. I knocked over my desk and physically attacked Saget. He didn't hold it against me, but in order to avoid a scandal and not raise too many questions, he gave me a sixty-day layoff. With an obligation of psychological follow-up. I didn't mind too much: I was mostly angry at the system. I didn't want to make the wrong enemy."

"Our enemies are those who break the law, Michael, not the system," said Assia.

"How do you explain the fact that a guilty man is still roaming free, after having assaulted at least four girls?"

"You don't know that, Michael."

He sat up abruptly and his tone changed. "I saw the panties hidden in his house, they were his trophies!" he shouted.

She rubbed Michael's back with the palm of her hand. Her soothing caresses seemed to calm him a little. She took advantage of it and said in a soft voice, "If this happens again, we will be there to pick him up and make sure that he will never do it again."

"Except for that to happen, there has to be a new victim... at least one," he retorted with a sad sigh. "We had the opportunity to stop him before he did it again, but we didn't."

"You're the one who crossed the line that time, Michael."

A heavy silence settled in the room, like an awkward guest.

Michael pushed aside the quilt and got out of bed. "I'm going to take a shower," he said coldly.

The sound of water coming from the bathroom mingled with that of the pelting rain that darted down the slopes of the roof. Assia lay on her back and inhaled deeply, taking in the scent of the room. She smiled; only the night witnessed it. Darkness poured in through the slanted windows like black ink, making all the objects and furniture in the room look ominous.

Michael's meditation corner suddenly seemed gloomy, and she thought of The Children of Gaïa cult and the years of mental and physical abuse he had experienced there.

Her gaze suddenly lingered on the telescope at the back of the room. Its orientation was odd to her, and her cop instincts were aroused.

Why wasn't it pointing to the sky?

She turned her head in the direction of the bedroom entrance, the sound of the shower still coming through. She stood up slowly, walked over to the instrument and put her eye to the end of the viewfinder.

In such weather conditions, she didn't expect to see anything, but she was surprised to be able to make out in the distance, on the other side of the lake, a pleasant green park lit by streetlamps diffusing a yellow halo. To the right of it, a large building with dark wood siding stretched along a gravel driveway. Further upstream, a sign illuminated by a powerful spotlight was battered by the powerful winds.

With each gust, Assia could see the inscription etched on it. She immediately recognized the letter G from The Children of Gaïa logo.

At 6:00am, her alarm clock woke her from a deep slumber. She felt the warm body of her lover against her and smiled.

Outside, the scenery was apocalyptic. It was raining non-stop, and the daylight was so dim that she could hardly tell what time of day it really was. Like an ill omen, an ominous mist hung over the lake, and the surrounding trees and fields were soaked.

"Already up?" Michael suddenly said, his eyes still closed.

"I have to go home and change before going to the station. I'll meet you there, okay?"

He was dying for a kiss before she left, but he froze, barely able to give her a smile.

On the floor below, the cats came running to Michael the moment he stepped into the big room. He noticed that a third cat had joined those who had spent the night. He distributed the food into several bowls, and made a mental note to stock up on kibble the next time he went shopping.

A series of short, repetitive sounds drew him to the large bay window in the living room. The beauty of the show outside moved him. The elements were unleashing to the rhythm of the gusts like the musicians of a symphony orchestra playing a cadenced score. A fleeting thought crossed his mind: who could be directing all of this?

Again, three sharp knocks on the glass pane. He searched the space in front of him, and down on his right, he finally saw what it was all about. A raven, sublimely black, was tapping the bay window with its beak.

Michael rushed to open the window and the bird darted inside. He noticed its slightly twisted right wing and recognized his old patient, the one he had tried to save two weeks earlier. He couldn't help but give a rare and genuine smile.

The three felines looked away from their bowls and approached the bird with hushed steps, like an elegant pack of wolves with slender bodies. The raven spotted the maneuver and spread his wings with a cawing sound, which made the frightened cats flee.

Michael inspected the raven more closely, and the bird remained still. The broken bone had healed with a slight defect, which did not seem to hinder it from flying.

He rummaged in one of the cupboards and came across the food he had prepared for the raven during its recovery. He poured it into a plate and the black bird threw itself upon it.

As moved as if he were reunited with an old friend, Michael sat cross-legged on the cold tile floor of the living room, watching this beautiful bird, considered by scientists to be the most intelligent of its kind.

The flow of his thoughts was interrupted by the vibration of his cell phone.

It was a message from Assia, who was already at the station. He made a quick mental calculation and realized that the forty-eight hours of custody of their suspect would end this morning.

He hurriedly finished dressing and left his home. The early winter temperature slid under his jacket like a cold blade. He shoved his hands into his pockets and his fingers brushed his tube of anti-anxiety medication. A slight shiver ran down his spine.

He turned around. With a hesitant gesture, he put the painkillers in a kitchen drawer and slammed it shut. The sound echoed through the room and he took one last look at the bay window. The raven had flown away.

26

Michael drove his car through the entrance gate and into the station parking lot, which was just beginning to fill up. On the way, he passed a van and saw Boris sitting in the front passenger seat. The tall blond looked at him with eyes as black as the sky above them.

Inside the station, he met Emma in the lounge over coffee. He felt a sudden rush of heat, and for a moment he thought he would faint. He took a hot sip and felt the caffeine coursing through his body. The tremors in his hands subsided.

"Are you all right?" Emma asked, looking worried.

"I'm fine. Just a little tired."

"You bet! We've been going home super late for two days and every time, we've had to be back here at dawn!"

"Where's Boris going?" Michael asked. "I saw him leaving in one of the vans."

"He's bringing Tremblay to the DA for the end of his custody."

Michael clenched his jaw, then took another drink from his plastic cup.

"You just missed his lawyer," Emma resumed.

A shadow seemed to cover Michael's eyes. "What?" he thundered.

"Beautiful blonde perched on heels, straight hair, full lips, super-strict look: a bombshell!" Emma replied then she bit her fist.

"How come Christopher Tremblay lawyered up?"

"He didn't call anyone, she just showed up."

"I don't get it. She just said she was Tremblay's lawyer? Nothing more?" Michael asked, frowning.

"Man, you should have been here! I've been working my ass off for more than an hour," she shouted. "What do you want me to say? Yes, she introduced herself as Tremblay's lawyer, but I told her that we had just sent him to the DA and she left."

"Did she leave a card? Anything? Did she say who hired her?"

"You know, lawyers..." Emma commented before chewing on her spoon.

Michael put this strange information aside and decided, as things stood, to focus all his energy on solving the case.

He took a deep breath. "Anything new on the cell phone numbers?" he continued.

"It's still a little early, but we should have it by noon, I hope."

"Yeah, when it's too late."

She put a hand on her colleague's shoulder. "Mike, we can't keep this guy here much longer, you know that. Are you worried about letting him loose?"

The case suddenly ran through his mind in flashes. This man was an enigma, a puzzle Michael had not been able to solve, even with all the help in the world. He found it hard to accept. Christopher Tremblay was going to win the chess game he had initiated.

A new sense of unease forced Michael to sit down. He tried to focus his mind on his breathing, but he wasn't alone: he had to put on a show. He turned his thoughts to his conversation with Emma. "Let's talk about these anagrams," Michael resumed, without much conviction in his voice. "Do you have any idea what could have caused the victims to hide their true identity?"

After a short pause, the young woman answered. "Witness protection program, maybe?" she said.

"Saget also suggested this."

"Did you go see Saget? Did you talk to him about the case?"

Michael massaged his temple and closed his eyes. "Yes, I needed his expertise," he explained.

"And he thinks the same thing?"

"He thinks that if we can't find any information on these people, that probably means it's classified."

"But we haven't come across classified documents, we just found, well, nothing, which is a little different," Emma said. "It all comes back to the cult, then..."

"I know," Michael replied, opening his eyes again, his face twisted into a grimace of pain.

"Are you sure you're okay?"

"Just a spot in my stomach," he lied.

"You and your rabbit diet!" she said sarcastically.

New grimace, between laughter and pain this time.

"I think it's this coffee," Michael managed to say after breathing in heavily.

The two officers left the room and entered the open space where, even at this early hour, nearly three quarters of the workstations were occupied by colleagues on the phone or staring at their screens.

With a wave of her hand, Emma signaled to Michael that she

was going back to her office. He followed her lead and slumped back in his chair. He took a few seconds to look around the room. The images that flashed across his retina were unfolding in slow motion, like a movie with a poorly calibrated film. His breathing became more staggered, and he had the sensation of running out of oxygen in spite of the deep puffs of air that he inhaled. His chest was heaving faster and faster, and the sounds he heard seemed to come from the bottom of a well. If he didn't pull himself together immediately, he was going to lose consciousness in the middle of the station.

He closed his eyes and visualized his Rubik's cube, as if in a three-dimensional digital animation. He began to rotate the sides slowly, trying to imagine every possible combination. This technique had always been effective and, once again, it proved to be so.

After seconds that seemed like hours, his heart rate returned to normal and a few drops of cold, salty sweat – the only evidence of his discomfort – dripped onto his desk. He had probably made a big mistake in weaning himself off his anxiolytics so abruptly. He was, however, keen on this kind of radical method. The day he had sworn that no living being would ever have to suffer again because of his food preferences, he had stopped eating meat and dairy products overnight. The same went for alcohol. He didn't believe in the technique of gradually reducing his consumption.

At that very moment though, his general condition was beginning to prove him wrong. In the battle between the chemical molecules and his willpower, the drugs had won hands down. *For this round only*, he thought.

Through the large windows of the station, Michael saw the van returning. One moment later, Lieutenant Pavlowski entered the precinct. A bad feeling crossed Michael's mind. He was coming back alone.

"Where's Tremblay?" Michael called out across the open space.

"Good morning to you too, Monroe," the tall blond man replied. "He was taken to the DA, and served with a notice that his custody was over."

A nervous lump formed in Michael's stomach and he walked around his workstation to approach his superior, taking slow, measured steps, like a wolf going to meet the leader of the pack. "And that's it?" he asked in a calm voice.

"The usual. A quick hearing and he was released under judicial supervision," said Boris.

An electric shock twisted his insides, but Michael clenched his teeth to keep his mouth shut. "He was placed under judicial supervision? You can't be serious. We're talking about four crimes with confession."

"No bodies, no one reported missing, names that are obviously fake... Do you want me to go on, Monroe?" Boris asked.

Michael shook his head and pounded his fist on the nearest desk. The noise echoed throughout the space and a dead silence ensued. All eyes were on him.

It was like *déjà vu*.

Pavlowski remained impassive and stared at his colleague coldly.

An intense heat was burning in Michael's heart and spreading to all his limbs. He suddenly ran out of oxygen but, on the way back to his desk, he managed to take a deep breath. He tried to ignore everything around him, concentrating his thoughts on his breathing.

Under the worried eyes of the policemen in the open space, Michael sat down with difficulty and closed his eyes to chase away the parasitic thoughts that were bouncing around in his brain.

With three long cycles of inhalation and exhalation, calm came over him. His hands were still shaking and he decided to occupy them with his favorite pastime. He reached for the handle of one of the drawers and pulled it towards him.

Roughly stuck to his Rubik's cube with a piece of clear tape, a picture he knew very well almost made him flinch. His heart seemed to miss a beat as he read the message, which was carelessly written in black marker.

On the glossy paper, Henry Saget and his mother paused smiling; Michael, on the right, only a few years old. The three handwritten words hit him hard in the gut, like an unscrupulous boxer looking for a knockout at any cost.

Mom and Uncle?

The room began to dance around him and his face twisted into a frightened grimace. Blood rushed to his temples, overloading his eardrums with pounding sounds. The tremors of his whole body redoubled, and he could not repress a cry which tore through the relative silence.

With a look of unquenchable anger, his eyes bulging and bloodshot, he stood up, grabbed his computer screen with both hands and threw it across the workspace. It crashed to the ground between two desks, missing the head of one of his colleagues by a few inches.

A few cries of protest and surprise went up, but Michael, with his muscles contracted and breathing heavily, was obviously not done yet.

Like a volcano that had been dormant for too long, he

unleashed his fury on all the objects in front of him, sweeping them away with his forearm. He violently kicked his desk and the heavy piece of furniture fell over with a racket of metallic creaks and cracking wood. Emma called for her friend to stop with a cry of distress that he did not hear. Michael sounded like a wild, bloodthirsty beast that had just been released from its cage after months of captivity.

He ripped out one of the drawers and threw it against the wall behind him, leaving a gaping hole in the plaster.

"Stop it!" Boris shouted.

Michael froze, clenched his fists and stared at his superior, his eyes lit up with flames of rage.

The two policemen watched each other for a long time, and when Michael dared to take a step forward, Pavlowski threw himself at him.

A powerful kick made Michael collapse on the floor. He barely had time to catch his breath when the imposing body of Boris was already diving on him, both arms in front. The tall man quickly seized the wrist of his colleague, pushed his shoulder violently to turn him on his belly and, in an instant, Michael found himself face against the ground, blocked in an armlock.

Boris pulled Michael's hand a little higher between his shoulder blades and he let out a painful howl. He approached his face near his colleague's, and whispered: "It's over, man. It's the end of the road for you."

The swinging doors of the room flew open and Assia rushed to meet the two fighters.

"What the fuck is going on here?" she shouted.

She threw a glance around her and analyzed the damage. Her lover was lying on the ground, in the middle of what looked like the aftermath of a grenade explosion.

In a split second, she understood what had happened. "Pavlowski, Monroe," she said, "my office! Now!"

As she nervously left the room, Michael calmed down and Boris released his grip.

The two men stood up and Boris grabbed the back of his colleague's neck. "You going to behave?"

Michael pushed him back impetuously to release himself from his hold, and everyone around believed that a new crisis of violence was going to start again. But Michael's anger was gone. The fire within him was certainly not extinguished, far from it, but the irresistible urge to vent his rage had diminished significantly.

He took several deep breaths and gave Emma an apologetic look. Somewhere deep down, he was ashamed that she had seen him like this again. He ran a hand through his hair and noticed that he was bleeding from a shallow cut he had picked up in the fight. He wiped the blood off on his thigh and headed for Assia's office. Boris followed him, and a few moments later they found themselves sitting across from the furious station chief.

She was seated, with her arms crossed and she was jiggling her foot nervously. Her brows were furrowed. She let a long minute go by, glaring at her man. "Do you think my station is a zoo?" she finally let out.

Pavlowski was surprised to be included in the sermon, but remembered that she knew nothing of the events that had taken place a few feet away from her.

"Boris, tell me what happened," Assia said.

The tall man cleared his throat. "I was just back from the DA's office and Detective Monroe asked me where our suspect was in a rather accusatory tone. I told him that he had been released. Then he punched the nearest desk. I imagine that he...

"I'm not looking for comments," Assia said, cutting him off dryly, "just lay out the facts."

He took the blow and resumed. "Detective Monroe then walked back to his workstation and, in a violent outburst, he threw everything in front of him, including the desk."

Assia sighed. "How did you end up the way I saw you two when I entered the open space?"

"Seeing that he wasn't going to calm down any time soon and that his anger was escalating, I decided to intervene and subdued him by tackling him to the floor," Boris replied.

"Michael, is that what happened?" she asked, turning towards him.

Without loosening his gritted teeth, he nodded. He felt the weight of her stare on him, but did not dare to cross it.

The only small hope he could hold on to was the fact that neither she nor Boris had been there during his very first crisis, the one that had earned him his long layoff.

Assia pivoted to face the back of the room, a reflex she had developed in her old office, where a window that looked out onto the outside allowed her to escape for a few moments from her life as a cop. When she had important decisions to make, she would indulge in this ritual. She felt almost ridiculous to find herself facing a bare wall that she hadn't even had time to decorate. Her anger went up a notch.

She turned around and looked at the two men. "Thank you, Boris, you can go now."

Pavlowski pushed back his chair noisily and left. He was disappointed that he was not going to be able to attend what was on the verge of happening in his boss's office. He would have loved to see Michael Monroe's face crumple when she announced the bad news. For Boris, there was only one way to close this incident.

Once he had slammed the door, Assia took her place opposite Michael. "What got into you?" she asked in a softer voice, and he could feel the anger lurking deep inside.

Michael remained silent, staring at the ground, his breathing still rapid.

"Do you realize what's hanging over you, Michael? You leave me no choice."

He raised his face, his brown eyes probing Assia's. "Do what you have to do," he said at last in an almost inaudible whisper.

"Damn it, Michael," she whispered while shaking her head as a heavy silence was imposed between the two lovers. The verdict fell like a guillotine blade. "Well, you are suspended from now on, until the decision of a disciplinary council which I will convene over the next few days. Before leaving the room, hand me your badge and your service weapon."

He had expected it; he had humiliated himself in front of all his colleagues a second time, and he was not surprised by the outcome. He couldn't blame Assia, she was forced to establish her authority in a male-dominated environment. Who would still respect her if she tolerated this kind of behavior within her department?

Eventually, more worried about the case than about his own fate, Michael dared a few words before leaving. "And the investigation?" he asked.

"Your colleagues are very competent, you can trust them and go back home to rest," she concluded without a glance.

27

With his hands gripping the steering wheel like a vice, Michael was speeding down a soggy road. Rain was pouring again.

He had dropped his gun and badge in Assia's office before slamming the door and exiting the precinct. When he had gone back through the open space to retrieve his jacket which was still lying on the floor, he had not deigned to glance at any of his colleagues. Nor had he agreed to pick up the various objects he had thrown across the room or to put his desk back in order. He did, however, feel a twinge of guilt when he thought of Emma. What would she think of him now?

He shook off these thoughts and focused on his new goal. Despite the fact that he was temporarily no longer a cop, he couldn't accept the idea that the possible perpetrator of four murders was roaming free. He had to find Christopher Tremblay at all costs.

To do so, he didn't have many options. Only one, in fact. He needed to go to a social shelter a few miles away, where all the homeless that were released by the police landed. It was a safe bet that the suspect was no exception to this rule.

A few minutes passed before a gray and sad building emerged at the end of a road whose many potholes were full of water, like miniature lakes overflown by the raging elements. Michael slowly drove his car to the front of the shelter. Without his badge, his police jacket would have to do.

He approached the reception desk and offered his most artificial smile to the young woman behind the counter. "Hello ma'am," Michael said, falsely affable, "we just brought you a man by the name of Christopher Tremblay, and he's missing some personal effects that I'm in charge of bringing back to him."

"Uh yes," she said, returning his smile, "but he left already."

Michael felt as if he had just been hit with a right hook. "He just left on his own? Do you know if anyone picked him up?" he asked.

"No idea," she replied. "You'll have to check with my colleague, but she's currently on a break. Do you want me to call her?"

He clenched his fist and swallowed the urge to smash it on the counter. "That won't be necessary, thanks anyway."

The front desk agent frowned and called out to Michael as he reached for the front door handle. "Weren't you supposed to bring him some stuff? You can leave it with us and we'll give it to him when he comes back."

Michael did not turn around and continued on his way to his vehicle, speeding up as soon as he was no longer sheltered from the rain. Finally alone in his car, he let out a cry of rage and slammed the wheel repeatedly.

The minutes seemed to stretch on endlessly while he remained without moving, eyes staring into space, his only companion the noise of the drops which struck his windshield at a chaotic rhythm. He thought again of the sexual abuser he had not been able to keep in the nets of justice either. Flames of rage were boiling inside him and shading his judgment. He wanted to explode, to throw it all away and run screaming into the storm; but he tried to pull himself together and think.

With concern, he looked at his trembling hands and searched the glove compartment for some kind of painkiller. Nothing. He had thought he was stronger than the drugs and that his body would resist the temptation to resort to anxiolytics. He had been wrong: one does not become sober overnight.

He closed his eyes and visualized the whole thing. Intrusive thoughts crossed his mind from all sides, but he tried to accept them, then let them go, which gave him a few short minutes of respite.

Suddenly, at the end of the tunnel, there was a glimmer of hope. He reached into his jacket and grabbed his phone. The cyber technicians had discovered that a number with a Canadian area code had contacted the four victims' cell phones in succession. That number was his last chance.

Michael fumbled with the numbers on the screen and pressed the call button. During the first few rings, he took several deep breaths.

No one picked up, but he was redirected to voicemail: *"Hello, you've reached Dr. Becker. I can't answer your call right now, but..."*

Click.

Michael hung up, he didn't need to hear any more.

For almost an hour, his car sped through the curtain of rain as the engine roared. Michael's heart rate seemed to be synchronized with the needle on the RPM gauge.

As he neared his destination, he slowed down and tried to calm the storm inside him. He finally turned onto the gravel road that led down to the harbor.

Once outside, he mechanically put his hand on the holster on his belt and felt a void that made him flinch. Michael didn't let this detail hold him back and made his way down the footbridge and onto the deck.

The bursts of adrenaline his heart was pumping throughout his body with each beat took away his tremors and the sense of loss. His senses were now sharper and he could focus on his task. He didn't bother to knock and entered the cabin unannounced.

The living room was empty and he hurried to the kitchenette at the bottom right, down some steps. He opened a cupboard and searched a drawer. He finally found what he had come for.

Suddenly, a door slammed at the other end of the room and Louis Becker appeared. "Is anyone here? Ingrid, is that you?" he asked.

Michael jumped out of the small kitchen, a butcher's knife in his hand, his gaze threatening and his jaws clenched.

The psychiatrist's mouth gaped, his eyes widened and, with a grimace of fear, he raised both palms in the air as if he were being held at gunpoint. His ribcage heaved, but no sound came from his throat; he stood there, frozen like a statue.

Holding the blade in front of him, Michael approached him slowly. "Sit down," he growled.

"But I... what the...?"

Becker took a few steps to the side and slid down the seat, both hands still up in the air.

Michael grabbed a stool and took a seat across from him. "Show me your cell phone!"

"O... Okay," Louis stammered, "it's in my pocket."

"Take it out and put it on the table in front of you," ordered the detective.

The psychiatrist complied with a trembling gesture.

"Put your hands down!" shouted Michael.

"What are you...?"

"I'm the one with the knife, I'm the one asking the questions! Yesterday, late afternoon, you called four phone numbers, remember?"

Becker's shoulders dropped a few inches and he sank into the cushion of the bench. The question almost seemed to relieve him. "If you're asking me this, you already know everything," he said without hesitation in his voice.

"No, I don't. I came here seeking answers," said Michael.

"The people I called... they're my patients."

The doctor was calm now, but the policeman watched his every move.

"Why didn't you tell us about this yesterday, when I came here with my colleague?"

"About my patients?" he answered quickly, frowning. "You asked me about Christopher Tremblay, not about my other patients; besides, you know that's the kind of information a doctor doesn't share."

The old man was clever, and Michael didn't like the turn the questioning was taking. He felt like he was gradually losing the upper hand. He slammed his fist on the table and Becker was startled. "Don't be a smart-ass!" he shouted. "By now, your patients are either corpses or trapped somewhere between life and death. So speak now, tell me everything you know, and fast!"

"I don't know anything more, I..."

"Why did you call them? Why them in particular?"

"I was afraid something had happened to them because of Christopher," said Becker.

The psychiatrist's non-verbal language indicated to Michael

that he was telling the truth, but his gaze was going surreptitiously back and forth to his right as he was speaking.

"What links Tremblay and the other four patients?" asked Michael irritably.

The name caused Becker to glance quickly to the side again, just as he had done without realizing it when he said the suspect's first name.

Suddenly, Michael heard noises coming from the room to his left. He jumped up from the stool and held the knife inches from the psychiatrist's face.

"You're not alone?" he said.

He didn't have time to answer; muffled, moaning-like sounds were coming from behind the door. Michael rushed to the handle and he opened it, still holding Becker at bay with his knife.

What he saw in the Captain's bedroom took his breath away. Lying on a carpet on the floor, was Christopher Tremblay, headphones on, writhing around – like a maggot on a hook – whimpering.

Seemingly out of his trance, he opened his eyes and saw Michael. A long cry of horror escaped his mouth, and the doctor shouted from the other room. "Leave him alone!"

As Becker took a few steps toward him, Michael entered the room completely and locked the door behind him.

At the sight of the knife, Christopher's face contorted into a grimace of terror and he rose on his elbows to crawl to the back of the room. When the back of his head hit the bed frame, he knew he was trapped.

Michael's eyes opened wide and his eyebrows arched, giving him the look of a monster ready to pounce on his prey. His lower jaw dropped, leaving a gaping mouth from which no sound came. He took a few steps, threw the knife behind him and jumped on the Canadian.

The detective slammed his head on the lacquered floor of the room, and put his two powerful hands around his neck. Christopher let out a scream that alerted Becker, still on the other side.

Worried and unable to witness the scene, the psychiatrist pounded on the wooden door panel with all his might, visibly increasing the sense of panic that was gripping Tremblay.

Michael, his mouth twisted, brought his lips to one of his prey's ears. "Speak!" he spat. "Speak now, damn it! Tell me what you did with the people on your fucking list!"

A fire of fury blazed in his eyes, and with each sentence Michael shook Christopher's throat as if he were a rag doll. With every jerk, the suspect's skull hit the ground with violence; but all Michael's rage and will were not enough to make him confess. He stayed silent, his wide eyes staring blankly.

"Speak, damn it, speak!" Michael shouted so loudly that his eardrums were fit to burst.

The door was shaking under Becker's fists. Michael tightened his grip around Tremblay's throat, and he quickly ran out of oxygen and coughed, his tongue hanging out of his mouth as if trying to swallow some vital air. His face turned scarlet, his eyes rolled back and he was seized by increasingly violent convulsions. In a frenzy, Michael continued to strangle him.

When all of Christopher's limbs went completely slack, he knew he had gone too far. He withdrew his trembling hands from his victim's neck and observed them for a few seconds, as if they were two foreign bodies, two killers that he had not been able to control.

In a burst of lucidity, he stuck his ear against the chest of the dead man. Nothing. Not a sound, not a beat in his chest.

Realizing his crime, he let out a guttural scream that tore

through the air and, to this deafening din was added the sound of the door that the psychiatrist had just shattered.

Without paying attention to Becker, Michael placed his lips against those of Tremblay and blew to fill his lungs with air. Immediately, he applied cardiac massage, using all his strength to restart the heart.

It was then that an intense pain shot through his skull, and his vision blurred for a few moments. The Captain had jumped on him with all his weight and had thrown his fist in the direction of his temple.

Michael was thrown to the ground and his assailant rolled with him.

"You killed him! You killed him!" Becker shouted, shaking his head frantically.

His voice was trembling with grief as if he had lost a loved one, but Michael was not affected by this and retaliated with a right hook to the psychiatrist's jaw. The pain in his knuckles was piercing, but the blow had been so strong that Becker lost consciousness for a few seconds. Enough time for the detective to drag the unconscious man into the living room.

He groped for the pair of handcuffs – the only piece of his equipment he had not left with Assia – hanging from his belt on his back. He located a copper pipe that ran along the length of the room to a small radiator and slid the old man into the corner to cuff his wrist to it.

Weighed down by guilt, Michael dropped heavily to the floor. His ears were ringing, he could feel the blood pounding in his temples and all his limbs were shaking as if he was seized by cold. He tried to relax for a few seconds, then took deep breaths of air, the air that Christopher Tremblay would have needed.

This morbid thought brought him back to reality. He took out his cell phone and did what he did every time he was in doubt: he called his uncle, Henry Saget.

Between two rings, he glanced at Becker. He was still out. Or maybe he was faking it; either way, it didn't really matter.

"Hello?" said Henry, picking up.

"I'm in trouble," Michael declared in a sad whisper.

"What's wrong?" the ex-cop asked in a steady voice.

Michael felt his throat knot up and had to pause briefly. "I fucked up..."

"Pull yourself together and explain everything to me."

Henry's fatherly, almost reassuring tone comforted him somewhat. Maybe the former captain would have a solution to his problem. Henry always had a solution.

For a few minutes, Michael told him about the circumstances of the trap he had gotten himself into. Saget listened attentively and made no comment. When Michael was finally done, he simply gave him a list of things to do before he arrived.

Before hanging up, Michael whispered a sincere thank you to his uncle.

He ran into the kitchen and searched the cabinets for a rag and window cleaner, which he quickly found under the sink. He was busy wiping his fingerprints off the front door handle when he noticed a thud against the hull of the boat. He rushed outside to the deck and pulled the hood of his jacket down over almost his entire face. If he came across someone, he couldn't be recognized.

He tried to get as close as possible to the source of the sound he was having trouble identifying.

Suddenly, he heard a small engine start up. He reached the other side of the deck and saw a lifeboat moving rapidly away on the river, piloted by a spindly figure that made his blood run cold. He suddenly felt as if he was falling into nothingness again.

His pulse accelerated dangerously. Cold sweat was already

soaking his lower back as he pressed against the boat, nearly losing his balance several times on the soggy, slippery deck.

Down in the Captain's bedroom, only the debris scattered on the floor of the doorway bore witness to the struggle that had taken place there, for apart from the bed and the rest of the furniture, the room was empty.

28

———

Michael bolted from the boat and ran to his car. Hands shaking nervously, he reached into the glove compartment and grabbed a pair of compact binoculars. He rushed to the dock – which would give him the best view of the entire river – and breathlessly scanned the horizon.

The outline of Christopher Tremblay and his boat were visible through the icy showers. He was gliding along the green waves of the Niagara River like a ghost with a dark purpose. The detective observed the road that ran along the river and spotted a bridge in the distance. If he hurried, he could certainly reach it before the fugitive. His heart raced and he rushed to his vehicle. He jumped into the car and sped off.

The engine roared as Michael sped through the storm, splitting the curtain of rain that came down and hammered the bodywork. He made a few dangerous passes, ignoring the other drivers honking at him and finally saw the metal structure on his left.

He hammered the gas pedal and turned the wheel violently. The car skidded on the slippery asphalt, before the tires bit into the sticky steel of the bridge and Michael was able to regain control of the vehicle. He stopped in the middle and got out.

The small speedboat, seconds away from passing under the structure, was approaching at a fast pace. Michael climbed over the railing, then wiped his rain-slicked face before bending his head over the rushing water to assess the situation.

Christopher looked up at him and, suddenly panicking, tried to maneuver around the detective, who had already jumped. He was not fast enough.

Michael fell heavily on top of him and he thought he heard a bone break. Tremblay screamed in pain, but was able to land a strong blow of the heel that sent the detective reeling backwards and off balance.

As the boat drifted away at full speed, its two passengers got up simultaneously. For a second, suspended in time, their gazes met. One was devoid of all humanity and the other was bloodshot, seemingly burning with the fire of hatred. Tremblay's left arm hung limply along his body, and Michael deduced that he had suffered a fracture.

The officer braced himself, spread his hands and threw himself forward. Despite his injury, Tremblay was quick enough to avoid the first strike and slid against the side of the hull. Using his good arm, he grabbed a wooden oar lying on the deck and, as Michael leaped back on top of him, he made a large circle in the air and struck his head.

A bolt of pain shot through Michael's skull and he thought for a moment that he was going to pass out, but the icy showers that fell on him kept him awake. He lost his balance, however, and had to catch himself at the stern.

Tremblay threw his makeshift weapon overboard and Michael was thrown off balance by the move. He realized why, a split second too late.

The fugitive had rushed to the throttle and pushed it with a jerk. The engine's propeller violently thrust the boat forward and Michael was thrown backwards.

He fell overboard into the muddy waters of the Niagara River, and when he resurfaced, he had to face the fact that he could not catch up with Tremblay.

As the boat moved away, an icy mass penetrated his clothes and weighed him down, hampering his efforts to stay afloat. He had to get back to shore as soon as possible.

In this part of the river, the force of the current was relatively weak, but sufficient to force him to exhaust himself a little more in order not to drift away.

After a few seconds, Michael could hardly feel his fingers, and his breathing became shorter and shorter. He suddenly had the impression that a frozen vice compressed his skull. The rain that poured into his eyes prevented him from seeing clearly, and he could only evaluate the distance that separated him from the edge with difficulty.

He used his last bit of strength to swim to the shore, reached out and finally felt a patch of soaked grass. He held on tightly to it and pulled himself up onto the shore with a groan.

Michael crouched down and tried to catch his breath and his spirits, but his tremors ruined the moment of rest. He needed to get active and get the blood flowing again in all his limbs.

He took off his jacket and rubbed his arms, shoulders, legs and face frantically then he looked around for some kind of shelter and found a spot a few feet away. He inspected his cell phone and assessed the damage.

At first glance, nothing seemed wrong, but soon the screen began to flicker. He noticed, however, that he had several missed calls from Henry and before his smartphone oxidized and froze forever, he had time to check the text message his uncle had left him:

Stop following Tremblay and get back to the boat! I'm with the shrink, he explained everything to me.

29

In the distance, a flash of lightning ripped through the sky and the tumult of the storm reached Michael's ears a few seconds later. He stood paralyzed for a moment, staring at the black screen of his phone, before shaking his head and repeating Henry's words over and over again.

What could Becker have said that Michael didn't already know?

He feared another ruse from the psychiatrist, and with a lump of anxiety in his stomach, he hurried back up to the bridge to get to his car.

By the time he reached his vehicle, it seemed to him that the rain had abated somewhat in intensity, but over the horizon, under the thick blanket of dark clouds, lightning laced the atmosphere with its electric claws. Thunder roared like an angry monster, announcing nothing less than a new storm.

Michael opened the trunk of his car and unpacked the contents of a duffel bag. He exchanged his soaked clothes for a pair of shorts and a T-shirt he used for his Sunday run. The outfit was certainly not adapted to the weather, but it was dry.

Chilled to the bone, he threw himself inside the car and

blasted the heat to maximum. A few seconds later, his tremors diminished and his face regained some color.

When he felt better, he turned the car around and headed for the Captain's boat.

Sitting on the bench, Henry was talking to the doctor, still handcuffed to the living-room heater in an uncomfortable position.

"Give me the keys, so I can set him free," said Henry, turning his head towards Michael.

"They're in my car. I want to hear him first, then we'll see," Michael replied in a cold tone.

"Michael, be reasonable," his uncle told him.

"Speak up, Becker! I'll untie you if what you say is worth it."

Henry could see the determination in his nephew's eyes, and he knew better than anyone that it was not necessary to insist in such cases.

The psychiatrist tried to sit up. "I've already told your uncle everything I know, but if you want the long version, we may be here for a while, and I don't know if..."

"I have plenty of time," Michael said, cutting him off.

The psychiatrist winced, massaged his wrist and began his story. "When Christopher came to St. John's, his initial psychiatric evaluation confirmed that of the court experts. Paranoid personality, manic delusional psychosis, bipolarity alternating between passive phases and extremely violent hallucinatory episodes. For these reasons, he ended up stabbing innocent passersby in the street. He heard voices that ordered him to rid humanity of the forces of evil. But after a few weeks under my watch, things didn't go quite as planned. The medical team and I found Christopher to be a sensitive, highly intelligent person, sometimes fiery and full of ideas, sometimes poetic and dreamy. It was then that I tried out a protocol on him that I had spent years developing. It was a blend of hypnotherapy, cognitive meditation, role-playing sessions; but also, very rigorous and technical drug dosage tests. This poor man had no family or friends, and therefore received no visitors. He was placed under the guardianship of the hospital which, in our research protocol, was quite practical and allowed us to move forward quickly.

"Then suddenly, a few months later, I met a young woman full of energy who wanted to live life to the fullest. She showed up two days in a row and then disappeared. A few days later, we met a somewhat tortured young man who liked to write poems and observe nature in silence. He did not stay very long either.

"For the next month, no one showed up, and Christopher became very aggressive toward the staff. We managed to calm his seizures with the right medication, but the dosage was still uncertain.

"Then one morning, as I was arriving at the hospital very early, I met another individual who turned out to be a real mathematical genius. That's when a pattern emerged in my head, and I wanted to understand..."

"Who are you talking about? What kind of fairy tale is this?" shouted Michael.

He jumped to his feet and approached the psychiatrist. Becker's discreet smile added fuel to the fire of his anger. "No more bullshit," shouted Michael. "Who are these people you're talking about?"

"Don't you understand?" Becker replied calmly.

Michael stood still.

"All of these people are Christopher Tremblay!" the doctor replied.

"What the..."

"Jenni, Colin, Slevin and Tod are all Christopher Tremblay."

A flood of information swirled in the detective's mind, and he squinted as if to better grasp it. Several elements resurfaced briefly: the fact that Jenni was a man, the anagrams; but he still had a hard time putting the pieces of the puzzle back together. "This story doesn't add up," Michael said. "The different cell phones, the different homes, the blood evidence at the scene... We're dealing with four different people!"

Becker shook his head. "Look, I don't have all the details of your investigation, but what you're telling me fits perfectly with what I'm about to tell you." The psychiatrist took a deep breath and continued. "When I understood that Christopher was suffering from a personality disorder and that several entities coexisted inside the same body, I had to identify them. Five very different profiles stood out: an extravagant young woman, a teenager with a passion for new technologies, a mathematical genius, an artist and, finally, the one we all know under the name of Christopher Tremblay. The first four personalities were completely crushed under the weight of Christopher's psychiatric disorders and paranoia. Hypnotherapy allowed me to bring them to the surface for a few hours each day and, when I was able to establish the psychological profile of each of the entities that cohabited inside him, I came up with the idea of a healing protocol.

"Christopher Tremblay's disturbed personality had to be buried deep within his consciousness, and to do this, his mind had to be completely locked down: it was imperative that he never be allowed any space for expression. This is why I helped the other individual personalities to emerge in a sustainable way. Each of them had to be fully developed and live their own lives to the fullest. We gave each one a new identity, and I found that an anagram of the name of the person who best represented them was an elegant start. Tod, the jack-of-all-trades artist, had always been fascinated by the composer Stephen Codman – whom he must have heard during Christopher's childhood while staying with one of his foster families in Canada – so we opted for the anagram Tod C. Sheepmann. It was kind of fun, and we kept it that way for the others. Jenni's name came from..."

"We know all that now," Michael intervened.

Becker's eyes widened in amazement. "Really? You found the origin of the anagrams? Hats off to you. And yet you couldn't figure out who Christopher Tremblay really was?"

Michael didn't appreciate the doctor's patronizing tone, but he ignored it, remembering that he was still slumped on the floor and trapped in his own living room. "I still can't figure out how this all came together," Michael wondered.

"It sounds complicated," Becker replied, "but it's actually quite simple. I set up a well-defined schedule for each of the personalities. That way, they could have a job, a place to live and fully exist. Colin, with his superior intelligence and interest in mathematical systems, set his sights on the stock market and its self-feeding and predictive models, which repeat themselves according to the psychology of the markets. He quickly became the financial guarantee of the entire group. His personality took control on Mondays and Fridays, days of intense stock market activity, and ensured a comfortable living for everyone. For convenience, a single bank account was maintained with the income that the various individuals earned from their occupations. Slevin proved to be an excellent online video game competitor. Thanks to sponsorships and donations, he, too, contributed substantially to the joint account. His days were Thursdays and, of course, Saturdays. For the rest of the week, Jenni appeared on Tuesdays and Tod, who needed time to compose, on Wednesdays and Sundays. Their ritual had to be followed to the letter, and the more solid and repetitive the routine, the deeper Christopher Tremblay's toxic personality was smothered, to the benefit of the other four."

Michael thought back to the elements he himself used in his meditation sessions: the lotus flower mat, the incense, the binaural sounds that force the brain into a semi-conscious state. "They used self-hypnosis to switch from one individuality to another, right?" the detective asked.

"Exactly!" said Becker. "I had to train them for months, but I wanted to have everything ready before Christopher came out. With this method, I was sure that nothing untoward would happen."

"Until two days ago..."

The psychiatrist suddenly put on a bewildered face. "What do you mean?" he asked.

"Your paranoid, violent Christopher Tremblay has done it again," Michael said gravely.

"I'm afraid I don't understand you at all," Becker said.

"We found blood at the homes of the four... personalities. Something happened that we're still trying to figure out."

Becker's expression changed dramatically, and he resumed his mischievous attitude and didactic, almost insolent, tone. "Don't you realize? It's *his* blood! He mutilated himself! I couldn't figure out how Christopher managed to resurface. I had him here in my room under hypnosis, and you came in with your big hooves and ruined everything!" Becker realized he was getting carried away and pulled himself together, instantly lowering the tone of his voice. "One thing is for sure though," he continued more calmly, "he has weakened all the other individuals to the point of physical damage and has regained control."

"Yet he confessed to killing those four people. He even listed them. Why?" growled Michael.

Henry Saget, who had been listening to them with a calm

and attentive ear until then, intervened. "Mike, maybe you could untie this gentleman now?"

While staring at the psychiatrist, Michael answered his uncle. "The keys are in one of my jacket pockets inside the trunk of my car. Go get them if you want; I'll stay with him."

Henry put on a heavy raincoat and went outside.

"I think I know why he did it," said Becker. "I'm pretty sure. He fears me, he fears my therapy, and he knows that I have the ability to completely stifle Christopher Tremblay's personality again, and hide him away forever. This has already happened to him once; it was his survival instinct that spoke. He turned himself in for the crimes to go to jail, but not in some psychiatric ward. He didn't want to be found. Christopher is not fully aware that the personalities cohabiting in his body are only emanations of his mind. He really thinks he has killed four people. To him, he belongs in prison. If you hadn't screwed this up, I would have known if Jenni and the others were still *alive*... If it's true, he's managed to get rid of them all..."

Becker's voice was shaking now and Michael saw a tear fall from his eye. "Years of work, years of research... all wiped out in a few hours," the doctor said, sobbing. "I don't even understand how Christopher came back to the surface." He pulled himself together and looked up at Michael again. "You say there was blood at the various homes? What else? Did Christopher say or do anything to explain his actions?"

"Some of the victims had GHB in them," Michael replied, "if you can call them that now... Tremblay wouldn't say anything except that one sentence he kept repeating: 'I killed them all.' He mentioned your nickname, *the Captain*, that's how I identified you, but you already know that. I can see why he was so afraid to see you again."

"Anything else?"

"Nothing special except that he had swallowed a key. It

opened a storage space in which we found all the cell phones of... Tremblay's personalities."

Becker's eyes widened and he sat up straight. "Did he? And what else was in that storage space?"

"Musical instruments and most of the furniture from Tod Sheepmann's apartment," Michael replied.

"Damn it, that's it!" shouted Becker as Henry returned to free him from his handcuffs.

The former Rochester PD boss helped him up and Becker sat on the bench, massaging the red mark on his wrist.

"So?" Michael asked.

"Christopher obviously chose the most fragile identity. Tod is a romantic, a hypersensitive man who suffers life rather than living it. He must have been planning his coup for years and took advantage of a moment of weakness on Tod's part to regain the upper hand."

Michael ran his fingers through his wet hair and scratched his temple. "The blood found at Tod's house was much older than at the others. Was it possible that he had completely overwhelmed Sheepmann's personality and taken control of his slot in their schedule, so to speak, without arousing the suspicions of the others?"

"That's exactly it!" said Becker. "He will have stifled Tod and let the ritual continue as if nothing had happened, reappearing on Wednesdays and Sundays in his place. Thus, he would have had all the time in the world to come up with a plan..."

Michael scratched his temple again and the frown on his face told the other two that he was searching his memory. "There's something else..." He paused for a moment.

"Yes?" Becker asked him.

"When Tremblay showed up at the Bloomfield police station, he had almost nothing on him but a business card with

The Children of Gaïa logo on it. What do you know about their connection to your former patient?"

"The Children of Gaïa, you say?"

"You heard me right."

"Honestly, I don't have any information about them," said the psychiatrist, shaking his head slowly. "Can you tell me any more?"

"Not really," said Michael. "He apparently attended a few meetings of an addiction support group. It's a kind of Alcoholics Anonymous type of organization run by the cult, and it serves as a front for recruiting future followers."

"In this case, I'm not surprised."

The hairs on the back of Michael's neck suddenly stood up. "Go on."

"Before his stay in my unit at St. John's, before he stabbed those people, Christopher went to all sorts of meetings like this. The voices he heard told him that the forces of evil were lurking among these poor people, drug addicts, alcoholics, etc. I'm sure he was attending several support groups in the area."

A huge weight suddenly seemed to lift from Michael's chest, the knot in his gut untangled a bit and he felt a deep sense of relief. He had been so overwhelmed and caught up in the connection to The Children of Gaïa that he had failed to see the obvious. Perhaps he had not dared to see the simple explanation that was offered to him. Christopher Tremblay was participating in discussion groups and it so happened that one of them was run by the cult that had haunted Michael's memories for years. If he looked a little deeper, he would surely find others, but did it still matter now that he knew everything?

As if freed from the weight of the world, the detective took a deep breath and his body relaxed. "Damn..." he let out as if he were alone in the room, "this guy is innocent," he whispered. "He didn't commit any crime..."

"On the other hand," the psychiatrist intervened, "his paranoid and violent personality is still a danger. We must get hold of him at all costs and..."

Michael grumbled, stiffened again and went out onto the deck. The floor was still wet, but the rain had stopped for a moment.

"Hey!" Becker shouted. "Where are you going?"

Without turning around, Michael walked onto the footbridge and said, "I'm going home for a hot shower."

Henry followed him and Becker rushed out of the cabin to shout at the two men. "You're a sick man, you know that? I won't let this go! I'm going to report you and your barbaric ways!"

Michael opened the door of his car and turned around. "Send your lawyer! I have a colleague who will be more than happy to receive their complaint."

EPILOGUE
TWO WEEKS LATER

Sitting on the terrace of a lakeside café, Emma and Michael were enjoying the gentle touch of the late spring sun. To their right, a large rock formation dropped steeply into the clear water, and to the left, the landscape stretched like a long silky ribbon, with colors ranging from emerald green to sky blue.

Michael reached for his glass of juice and took a sip. "So what's the good news?" he asked, breaking the silence.

"The complaint that Becker filed against you was dismissed," said the young woman, her face almost entirely hidden behind huge sunglasses.

"Is that so?" Michael asked.

"Legitimate defense considering the circumstances of the investigation in progress," Emma explained.

"I wasn't in service," he added, frowning.

"You must be in Jenkins's good books then. She *updated* your suspension to the following day." Emma leaned over her glass and sipped a little of her colored cocktail before resuming. "By the way, when are you coming back to the station?"

"In a month and a half, give or take. I got sixty days," he replied, sinking back into his seat to look at the horizon again.

"Sixty days? Again? That must be your lucky number! Jenkins seems to like you but she didn't want to be too easy on you."

Emma thought she saw a slight sneer form at the corner of her colleague's mouth, but she chalked up this little grimace to the dazzling sun.

In the distance, a sailboat gliding across the surface of the lake changed tack in an elegant maneuver. The laughter of children playing on the grass mingled with the cries of seagulls watching for fishermen on the pier, and people walking their dogs paraded past them on the jetty.

"No news from Tremblay?" Michael suddenly asked in a more serious tone.

"I haven't heard anything. You know, we all tried to forget about it quickly after you contacted Jenkins to explain everything. It's possible that we felt a little ashamed... We'd put so many cops and resources into this case... I can't believe this guy is still out there."

"*C'est la vie!* He didn't commit any crime."

"You know very well that if the guy's got paranoid violent behavior, he's going to go after someone one day, that's for sure. The question is when?"

"Don't make assumptions, Emma. Tremblay is an innocent man; he doesn't belong in prison."

She straightened up and grinned at Michael. "Ladies and gentlemen, mark Detective Monroe's words because it's a first!" she said, punctuating her sentence with a playful laugh that made Michael smile. "By the way," she resumed, "do you remember the guy you booked under rape suspicion, the panties collector? Some colleagues from another precinct raided his new place and found some pedophile videos on his computer."

Suddenly captivated, Michael straightened up and brought

his face close to his colleague's. He had the most serious look on his face. "How do you know that?"

"After what happened with you, the guy moved to Buffalo. I have an acquaintance working at the Buffalo PD."

"An acquaintance, you say?"

"Anyway," Emma replied, blushing, "your panty collector is in for a real treat there."

Michael lowered his gaze for a few moments and resumed a comfortable position in his seat. Emma could have sworn that he had a satisfied look on his face.

After a while, he glanced at his watch and sighed.

"Okay, I get it!" Emma shouted with amusement. "You're not the only one having a date here, you know. As soon as I'm done with my cocktail, I'll leave you alone with your mysterious rendezvous."

A few minutes passed and Emma noisily drained her glass, stood up, and gently kissed Michael's forehead. "I hope to see you before then, but if not, see you at the station, Mike."

"See you soon, my sweet redhead," he replied with a smile.

Emma walked away and disappeared among the tables and umbrellas on the terrace. When she reached her car on the small parking lot, she noticed a familiar vehicle crossing the gate and parked on one of the lots, at the back.

Eager to confirm her hunch, she climbed into the car and continued to spy on the scene through the dark lens of her thick glasses.

Captain Assia Jenkins, radiant and sexy, was heading towards the terrace that Emma had just left. Driven by curiosity, she couldn't help but stretch her neck over her car door to observe her boss.

When the tall, dark-skinned woman reached Michael's table, he stood up, smiled, and kissed her on the lips as if the world around them didn't exist.

THE END

A NOTE FROM THE PUBLISHER

Thank you for reading this book. If you enjoyed it please do consider leaving a review on Amazon to help others find it too.

We hate typos. All of our books have been rigorously edited and proofread, but sometimes mistakes do slip through. If you have spotted a typo, please do let us know and we can get it amended within hours.

info@bloodhoundbooks.com